Three Black Boys:

The Hotep Brother Manuscript

ZANGBA THOMSON

Copyright © 2020 Zangba Thomson, Bong Mines Entertainment, LLC. All rights reserved.

ISBN-13: 978-0-578-67675-3

Library of Congress Control Number: 2019902951

Publisher: Bong Mines Entertainment, LLC

Bong Mines Entertainment, LLC

P.O. BOX 1745

North Baldwin, New York, 11510

Email: contact@bongminesentertainment.com

Please visit www.zangbathomson.com for more information about Zangba Thomson, or you can contact Zangba at Z@zangbathomson.com.

Please visit www.bongminesentertainment.com for additional information.

(**P**) Positive (**E**) Energy (**A**) Always (**C**) Creates (**E**) Elevation (**PEACE**).

TABLE of CONTENTS

Three Black Boys:
The Hotep Brother Manuscript

Barnes, Demus, and Baker are back with another actioned-packed adventure. This time, they travel to Monomotapa, Alkebulan, where the king and queen were recently slain by Ego, a familiar nemesis who the three Black boys thought they had destroyed in the afterlife. But they were deeply mistaken. Now, Ego has in his possession The Hotep Brother Manuscript, a sacred book filled with spiritual laws and enchanting spells, which he uses to turn the Monomotapan military into Egomaniacs. By his side is Deadra, a divine entity, and their goal is to rule Monomotapa and discontinue all shipments of gold to Planet Black, the home of the deities. Currently, the black planet is vulnerable, protected by a thin layer of gold that is quickly depleting. With the threat of an incoming meteoroid shower looming, there's no telling what might happen to Planet Black if a large shipment of gold doesn't arrive there soon.

Note to readers:

While reading "Three Black Boys: The Hotep Brother Manuscript," please be aware that these three asterisks * * * stand for a shift in focus, changes in characters, time, or topic.

CHAPTER 1

Ego's brain crystal, moments after the three Black boys deactivated its forcefield, rolled its way into the sea of lava, which is extremely hot and boiling at a temperature of 1200°C. However, the crystal, made of tungsten scheelite, maneuvers to the bottom of the sea of lava without dissolving. After searching for a while, it finds a tiny Blackbox, the size of a pill. The box belongs to Ego and serves as his backup hard drive, in case his essence needs to be restored. It takes some time, but the naturally intelligent crystal withdraws Ego's essence from the

Blackbox without any problems. Shortly afterward, the crystal spins swiftly in one spot until it produces enough friction to chisel its way through the hardened base of the sea of lava. The crystal, descending at a tremendous speed, free falls in darkness before escaping through an opened skyline. The crystal splashes into the inhospitable Black Sea, located in Eurasia, surrounded by Europe, Caucasus, and Anatolia. It sinks past fish and inconspicuous bacteria before crashing into the ground. The impact forms a huge mushroom cloud, which discharges an assorted array of colorful lights.

An inquisitive bluefin, searching for food, sees the shiny crystal and swallows it. Before the tuna can swim on its merry way home, a targeted harpoon pierces its four hundred-pound body. The fish struggles to wiggle itself free, but its efforts are in vain.

Maximus Schmeling, a middle-aged fisherman, stands on the deck of his boat. He's operating a launcher that's reeling in the captured tuna via a motor-powered rope. When the fish is safely onboard, he removes the harpoon from its body.

"This is the biggest tuna we've ever caught," Schmeling admits with great pride. "We can sell seventy percent of it and store the rest."

"I agree," replies Hannah, Schmeling's forty-five-year-old wife.

He tries to kiss her, but she turns her head.

"What's wrong?"

"I'm not in the mood."

"Are you okay?"

"Yes." But her eyes are watery.

Schmeling sees that she needs comforting. Therefore, he caresses her. "The doctors are wrong, you know."

"But it's been over a year now," she replies. "Maybe they're right. Maybe I'm too old to have children."

Schmeling doesn't like the words coming out of his wife's mouth. "We'll get a third, fourth, and fifth opinion if we have to."

But Hannah isn't buying that. Each moment, she sinks deeper in despair.

"What's the use, Max?" she questions her husband's optimism. "You picked a fruit from a barren tree."

"Don't say that."

"It's true. I'm not fertile."

"That's not true," says Schmeling. "You will have our baby. We just have to keep trying."

"For how long, huh?"

He kisses Hannah. "For however long it takes."

Schmeling picks up his knife and begins cutting off the tuna fins.

He asks Hannah, "Can you gut it while I put the fins on ice?"

She agrees.

He walks away, carrying the fins on hooks, and disappears below the deck.

Hannah grabs the knife and viciously shoves it inside the tuna's underbelly. With a strong swipe, she rips it apart. While removing the fish entrails, she spots the crystal sparkling in the sunshine. She stares at the object but doesn't know what to think of it as she picks it up.

"Hannah," a gentle voice says.

She looks around but no one is found.

"Hannah," the voice echoes.

Hannah swallows saliva. "Who said that?"

"You are holding me in your hand," the voice replies.

She opens her hand and sees the crystal.

The voice within it proclaims, "My name is Ego, a deity from the Great Unknown. I came here to help you."

"Help me?" She doesn't understand. "Help me with what?"

"Don't be afraid, Hannah."

"How did you know my name?"

"I know everything. I know you want to have a child. Am I right?"

Hannah is surprised. *How does this thing know that?* But what she doesn't know—that thing is an extraterrestrial entity that's reading her mind.

He tells her, "I can fertilize your eggs with my divine sperm."

Hannah swallows again. "I don't need your help."

"The doctors are right. You are too old to have a baby, and your Fallopian tube is damaged."

She takes a few seconds to think. It seems like an eternity. Finally, she asks, "How exactly can you help me?"

"Swallow the crystal in your hand, like you're swallowing a pill. No one will ever know how you got pregnant. Your husband already believes in miracles. Why not give him one to believe in?"

Hannah thinks deeply about Ego's enticingly risky proposition. He's right, she will never get pregnant the natural way. However, a supernatural birth might be her only opportunity to becoming a mother. After exhaling deeply, she swallows the crystal, hoping she has made the right decision. A few seconds later, a sharp pain spewing in her stomach causes her to grimace.

"Tomorrow, we'll go to see a holistic doctor," says Schmeling, resurfacing from below the deck. He walks over to Hannah, now crunched over in agony. "What's wrong?"

"I'm feeling nauseous."

"You need to rest. I think all this baby talk is starting to drain your energy."

"I think so too."

Schmeling picks her up and carries her below the deck. In their bedroom, he lays her on a bed covered with warm blankets.

Hannah grabs his hand. "Don't go. Stay with me a little while longer."

"But I have to finish gutting the tuna. If I don't, it will smell. Plus, I don't want to share our catch with flying scavengers."

She unbuttons her blouse. Her pointed nipples, mounted on her ripe breasts, causing him to rethink his statement. Before he can utter another word, his phallus stiffens, and a comforting feeling causes it to throb with passion.

He lays down with Hannah and kisses her pierced belly button, working his tongue up to her breasts and gripping them firmly.

Hannah breathes heavily, and her exotic moans turn him on. He shoves his middle finger inside her wet vagina and rotates it counter-clockwise, while she nibbles on his earlobe.

Schmeling pulls down his pants and shoves his bulging phallus inside Hannah.

She moans passionately. She takes his early strokes well, but after that, she's left in a vulnerable state. Her clitoris tingles. Seconds later, overwhelming joy travels throughout her body.

"Yes, yes, yes," she shouts repeatedly before experiencing an intergalactic orgasm.

Schmeling ejaculates also. His face looks pale while saliva drips from the side of his mouth. He rolls over, exhausted from unleashing the beast on his wife.

But she's still shaking, experiencing another orgasm. A gushy white substance leaks out of her vagina and runs down her inner thighs. He wipes the fluid with a towel and kisses Hannah, hoping a baby can come out of the lovemaking.

"I think you're right," says Hannah.

"About what?"

"About me getting pregnant," she replies. "I'm starting to believe it can happen."

Schmeling agrees. He stands, sweat dripping down his hairy chest. He feels like an adult film star, proud of his sexual performance. In the last couple of weeks, he's been lackluster. But a few minutes ago, he was nothing shy of spectacular.

He feels Hannah's skin—it's hot. "Looks like you're coming down with a fever."

"A fever to do it again." Hannah grabs his limped member, but it's down for the count. The referee has called off the fight.

Schmeling cops a plea. "I have to gut the tuna."

Hannah is disappointed. "Okay go," she says with an attitude. "Have fun gutting your tuna."

He leaves.

Hannah takes a deep breath and exhales. A warming sensation travels throughout her body. She knows she's pregnant because she feels something growing inside her womb.

* * *

Nine months later, Hannah screams inside a cabin in the heart of the Caucasus Mountains. She's in agony, strapped to a bed. Her legs are pulled far apart, her head throbs, and pain progresses through her body. Her vagina feels like it's being sliced open with a heated knife.

Schmeling looks worried. His beard is in desperate need of a trim. The sight of Hannah's bloody bed causes him to feel woozy, but he holds his ground.

A midwife, situated in a hiking position, is prepared to catch the baby. "Breathe," she tells Hannah, "and push!"

Hannah breathes and pushes but her strenuous attempts to push her baby out causes her uterus to tear significantly. Eventually, her baby is delivered in the midwife's hands, but Hannah has lost a significant amount of blood.

"It's a boy!" the midwife exclaims triumphantly.

Hannah is happy, but she is in too much pain to celebrate. As she loses more blood, she begins to feel lightheaded and cold.

Schmeling is warm with joy because he always wanted a son and now he has one.

"We won't clamp his umbilical cord yet," the midwife tells Schmeling. "Let's wait a few more seconds."

Schmeling agrees.

At midnight, the midwife clamps the umbilical cord and severs it. She wraps the weeping child inside a warm blanket and hands him to his father.

"What are we going to call him?"

Hannah replies, "Ego," before experiencing shortness of breath. Her heart, beating too fast, is unable to pump enough blood to the rest of her body. Plus, a lack of uterine muscle contraction causes her uterus to fail in contracting adequately. A short while later, she experiences a severe postpartum hemorrhage and dies in bed due to childbirth complications.

The midwife tries her best to resuscitate Hannah but she is unable to. Hannah is dead and gone, and no longer with them.

"Hannah!" Schmeling screams in anguish as he stares at his wife's deceased body. All she ever wanted was to have his baby. Now that she had accomplished that goal, it pains him to know that she won't be around to help him raise their son. So many negative thoughts are traveling through his mind, and he isn't able to think sensibly. Hannah would still be alive if it wasn't for him. Why did he have to impregnate her? Without rationale, he blames himself for her untimely death. But when he looks into his son's baby-blue eyes, all of his worries disappear.

* * *

Eighteen years later, Ego is all grown up. His manly face is chiseled and his blond beard is trimmed to perfection. He's dressed like a commander-in-chief of the army, and a passenger inside a commercial helicopter. His aging father, Schmeling, is seated beside him. Schmeling's face is wrinkled with experience and his head is decorated with thinning grey hairs.

The pilot lands the helicopter in a desert located on the outskirts of Monomotapa, Alkebulan. Sand swirls in the air, but after the propellers stop spinning, it settles.

Ego and Schmeling exit the helicopter. Ego is carrying a briefcase. They walk past several giant tree stumps with smooth tops and continue past a group of native excavators. Some of the diggers are using backhoes and other small tools to sift through dirt, and others are operating heavy machinery.

Meshi, the site's archaeological supervisor, walks over to Ego and Schmeling. "Greetings, and welcome to Alkebulan. What you asked for has been dug up. It awaits you."

Ego smiles and hands the briefcase to Meshi. "It's all there," he tells him. "You can count it if you want."

"That won't be necessary." A short while later, Meshi is leading his clients inside a torch-lit cavern, where a gold chest rests on top of a platform rock.

Meshi urges Ego to look inside.

Ego walks over to the chest and opens it; he's trembling with excitement.

"Behold," he says while staring at the content inside. "The Hotep Brother Manuscript." He picks up the ancient book and blows dust from its cover. After wrapping it in a cloth, he tells Meshi, "You can keep the chest. I do not need it."

Meshi is shocked. The chest is made of solid gold. Why doesn't Ego want to keep it? He concludes the answer doesn't even matter. Today must be his lucky day.

"Thank you," he tells Ego, his mind calculating how much he can sell the chest for.

Ego, Schmeling, and Meshi exit the cavern.

Sand swirls in the air as the helicopter propellers spin. Meshi shields his face while Ego and Schmeling board the helicopter. A short while later, Meshi sees his clients flying away.

* * *

The pilot lands the helicopter in a mysterious territory where animals and creeping things run for cover.

Ego and Schmeling exit the aircraft with Ego carrying The Hotep Brother Manuscript in his right hand. He tells the pilot, "Wait here, we won't be long."

The pilot nods in agreement.

Ego leads Schmeling into uncharted territory, where an ancient tomb is found. Its entrance is blocked by a stone, covered with spider webs and thick, green moss. Ego removes the webs and he and Schmeling roll the heavy stone out of the way. A few seconds later, they are entering the eerie tomb. A ghostly sound frightens Schmeling. But Ego keeps his cool, he isn't afraid.

"There she is," he says before walking over to a closed coffin, blanketed with spider webs.

"She?" Schmeling looks uneasy.

Ego opens the coffin slowly, looks inside, and sees Deadra's body. She looks just as beautiful now as she did when he last saw her. She hasn't aged one bit. Ego runs his fingers down her angelic face and smiles. After Mother Nature broke his heart, Deadra was there for him during his darkest hours, and that's why he has never forgotten her. He kisses her lips, knowing a divine kiss is the only thing that can wake her up from her sleep. A few seconds later, she opens her eyes and rises.

"Who kissed me?"

Schmeling takes a couple of steps backward, trying to take himself out of the equation. He doesn't want anything to do with what's about to happen.

"I did!" Ego confesses defiantly.

Deadra turns her attention to him.

He continues, "It's me, Ego."

Deadra recognizes his voice. "Ego?"

"Yes," he replies.

Deadra crawls out of her coffin and walks over to Ego. She touches his face. "You look different from how I remembered you looking the last time we were together."

"I will explain later. It's a long story."

Schmeling can't believe what he is witnessing—his son and Deadra kissing.

"What do you want?" Deadra asks Ego.

"For us to rule Monomotapa."

"That's an ambitious thought. You know we have enemies in high places. So tell me how? I'm curious to know."

Ego shows her The Hotep Brother Manuscript and she is shocked.

"How did you find it?"

"Eons ago, I peeked out of the sky and saw the lords hiding it in the Enchanted Forest, which is now a desert in Monomotapa. I had it excavated."

Deadra looks at Schmeling. He is frozen in fear, too scared to move a limb. This is not what he had signed up for. He thought he was helping his son find buried treasures, not summoning the dead.

Deadra returns her gaze on Ego, "The spells, how do they work?"

"Each spell is activated when two or more divine beings chant the spell in unison."

Ego opens the manuscript to page thirteen, revealing a spell written in the official language of Planet Black. He and Deadra recite the 'kundalini spell' in their native tongue. Moments later, nitrogenic energy enters Schmeling's body, transforming the elderly man into a small black crow.

Schmeling joyfully flies around the tomb and eventually escapes through the opened doorway. A few seconds later, he returns to the tomb and lands on Ego's broad shoulder. Ego pets Schmeling's new bird body with gentle strokes.

"Caw! Caw! Caw!" Schmeling says with three caws while flapping his wings. He tells Ego, "Thank you, my dear, son. Before I was feeble and old. Now, I am young, vibrant, and I have wings to fly."

Ego, pleased with his father's statement, exits the tomb in a happy mood with Deadra by his side. Outside, the sunlight is gleaming through the trees. Schmeling is riding on Ego's shoulder when they enter the helicopter.

The pilot is alarmed when he sees Deadra. The hair on his body stands on end. He looks around for Schmeling but doesn't find him. So he turns to Ego and asks, "Where's your father?"

"Right here on my shoulder," Ego answers.

The pilot swallows hard. He's frightened by Ego's and Deadra's intimidating looks, not to mention the coldness in Schmeling's little black eyes.

Ego opens the manuscript to page thirty-three. He and Deadra recite the 'every knee shall bow spell' in their native tongue. Moments later, a black cloud of nitro-genic energy enters the pilot's body, transforming the man into an Egomaniac.

* * *

The Precinct of Ra is heavily guarded by hundreds of foot soldiers who see a helicopter approaching. Some of them point guns at it, not knowing what to think of their unwelcome visitors. Also, they see a thick black cloud of nitro-genic energy hovering above the helicopter.

The pilot lands the helicopter inside the fortress. It doesn't take long after the propellers stop spinning for the soldiers to surround the helicopter, eager to see who's inside.

The nitro-genic energy that's hovering above the helicopter enters the soldiers' bodies. A few seconds later, they are transformed into Egomaniacs.

Ego and Deadra exit the helicopter with Schmeling riding on Ego's shoulder.

The black cloud of nitro-genic energy follows Ego and Deadra wherever they go.

The Egomaniacs bow their heads as Ego and Deadra are walking past them.

* * *

Inside King's Mansion, King Ujamaa, ruler of Monomotapa, sits on a six-feet-nine-inch throne, next to the Queen of Monomotapa. Looking stunningly beautiful, she is seated on a similar throne made of gold. Ujamaa is conversing with Matata, the captain of the royal guards—an elite group of military bodyguards responsible for protecting The Queen and Ujamaa at all cost.

Twenty-four royal guards are standing in strategic positions around The Queen and King Ujamaa.

One of the guards walks over to Ujamaa and whispers something in his ear.

Ujamaa is surprised. "Visitors? I'm not expecting any guests."

The huge iron door swings open. Deadra and Ego enter unannounced with Schmeling riding on Ego's shoulder. He flies upward and lands on an elaborate crystal chandelier decorated with sparkling red rubies. From there, he sees the action unfolding down below.

The cloud of nitro-genic energy enters Ujamaa's royal guards, transforming them into Egomaniacs.

Ujamaa is shocked to see Ego and Deadra walking towards him.

"Where are my guards? Why isn't anyone stopping them?" Ujamaa looks uneasy.

The Queen is equally as worried and shocked to see their soldiers gathered behind Ego and Deadra.

Ujamaa shivers in fear, even though he is a survivor of several coups. But this takeover is different. Masterfully won without anyone yielding a sword or firing a gun.

"What's going on here?" Ujamaa asks. His once demanding voice weakening. "Who are you? And what do you want?"

Ego orders Matata to shoot Ujamaa.

The captain, already an Egomaniac, brandishes his gun and drills numerous bullets into the king. Ujamaa is dead before his body hits the floor.

The Queen cries out loud, "Ujamaa!"

Ego orders Matata to shoot her.

He riddles The Queen's head and body with bullets, sending her into the afterlife. Her bleeding body is lying next to Ujamaa's corpse in a beautiful way.

After the mandatory bloodshed, Ego and Deadra seize the moment to address their army of Egomaniacs, still under the spell's influences.

"I am Ego, your new king!"

The Egomaniacs shout, "All hail Ego, the new King of Monomotapa, Alkebulan."

"I am Deadra, your new queen!"

The Egomaniacs shout, "All hail Deadra, the new Queen of Monomotapa, Alkebulan."

Ego orders several Egomaniacs to remove the two dead bodies and others to clean up the bloody mess. They do as they are told, and within an hour, the place is sparkling clean.

Ego and Deadra are seated on their thrones, and they are pleased.

Ego tells Deadra, "I won't be satisfied until we destroy Father Time and Mother Nature for what they did to us."

Deadra replies, "Destroy Planet Black and they will have nowhere to go."

"But how?"

"Put an end to the gold shipment from Monomotapa to Planet Black. Without gold, the black planet will be vulnerable to incoming threats such as the annual meteoroid shower."

Ego is pleased with her answer. He's happy, cheerier than he has been in a very long time.

A muscular Egomaniac, his fitted uniform hugging his body, brings over a golden birdcage and sits it at Ego's and Deadra's feet. The Egomaniac bows and returns where he came from.

"Caw! Caw! Caw!" Schmeling flaps his wings and flies into the cushioned cage. It's comfortable, and he's happy to have it.

* * *

After the celebration, Ego and Deadra take a much-needed road trip to a mountain region in Monomotapa. They are riding in the backseat of an armored jeep driven by an Egomaniac. Traveling behind them are three opened-top military trucks carrying large groups of armed Egomaniacs, dressed in olive-green army fatigue uniforms with dark matching green hardhats.

Schmeling is joyfully flying above the convoy.

When they arrive at their destination, they see several men guarding the entranceway to the gold mine. The men, dressed in black uniforms, are alarmed when they see Ego, Deadra, and the group of Egomaniacs approaching. The guards are unaware of King Ujamaa's and The Queen's deaths, and they know nothing about what's going on. As soon as Ego and Deadra get close to the entrance, the black cloud of nitro-genic energy enters the guards' bodies. A short while later, they are transformed into Egomaniacs, and they respectfully move away from the entranceway, allowing Ego and Deadra to enter.

Inside the gold mine, Ego and Deadra are wowed by the amount of gold they see. Enough to supply Planet Black for a very long time.

"That's a lot of gold," says Ego, with a huge smile on his face.

"Indeed it is," says Deadra. "Gold that will never find its way to Planet Black ever again. There's an empty warehouse attached to King's Mansion, we can stockpile the quarried gold there."

Ego agrees.

The black cloud of nitro-genic energy enters the mine and transforms everyone there into Egomaniacs.

CHAPTER 2

Barnes, Baker, and Demus are relaxing inside a spacious chamber within the Mothership. They are watching spacecrafts, stars, and asteroids float by. The brothers-in-arms are still shocked that they were successful in saving humanity from being destroyed. Defeating Ego and returning the melatonin cosmic tree to its proper place is their greatest accomplishment.

Barnes looks at his bluebird chime and remembers it annihilating Ego. He shakes the instrument, and an angelic sound resonates above a delicate noise being reproduced by a nearby solar generator.

"Every now and then, I think about Earth and all the fun we used to have," Barnes says with teary eyes. The nostalgic statement lingers for a moment before he continues. "I miss driving my Honda through our neighborhood during the nighttime. I miss, Mom. I think about her a lot. How she's doing? Who's taking care of her? I wish I was there, by her side. I wish I could see her again. Hold her hands and tell her how much I love her."

"I feel you, bro," says Demus. "I think about my parents a lot too, and their mental wellbeing. I know it wasn't easy for them to live a regular life after my death. I wonder what they are doing right now? Probably sitting in my bedroom waiting for me to come home."

"Y'all got me in my feelings right now," says Baker. "I ain't gon' lie, I think about my family all the time, and what life would have been like if we never committed that robbery. My bakery would probably have been opened by now, and I would have been the breadwinner in my family. Now, I can't even imagine the financial state my family is currently in. For all I know they could be living on the streets, begging for their next meal. I feel bad for thinking this way, I know I should be more optimistic."

Father Time and Mother Nature enter the chamber.

The three Black boys stand.

"I see y'all have gotten used to life after death," says Father Time, his blissful energy enveloped beneath his spiritual physique.

"Yes, I believe we have," replies Barnes. "I feel like a superhero living inside a science-fiction movie."

"That's good to know," says Mother Nature. "Imagination is better to have than silver and gold."

"Is everything okay?" asks Barnes.

"No," replies Mother Nature, her voice relax like the early morning sounds of nature. "An unnatural incident recently occurred on Earth."

"What happened?" asks Baker.

Father Time exhales deeply before answering, "Ego escaped."

"But how?" asks Demus. "We saw him getting liquefied in the sea of lava."

Barnes and Baker nod in agreement.

"Ego's body dissolved, but his brain crystal survived," replies Mother Nature. "It escaped through a tiny crack in the sky."

Barnes, Demus, and Baker don't know what to think. All they know is Ego's escape from the bottom of the sea of lava sounded brilliant.

"We don't know how, but Ego has a human body and an army of foot soldiers that he calls his Egomaniacs," says Father Time. "Also, he is the new King of Monomotapa, Alkebulan."

"What happened to the old king?" asks Demus.

"It didn't end too well for him and his wife," replies Father Time.

Mother Nature adds, "We want you to stop Ego before he becomes too powerful."

"But there's another problem," says Father Time, his voice peppered with concern. "Ego is not alone. He recited an ancient spell and raised the deity Deadra from her sleep. Together, they are a dangerously mighty couple. To destroy them, you must take away the source of their power."

"And what is that?" asks Barnes.

"The Hotep Brother Manuscript," says Mother Nature. "It's a sacred book filled with spiritual laws and enchanting spells. Ego excavated the book in Monomotapa, and we have reasons to believe he's using spells to control the Monomotapan military."

"So let me get this straight," says Barnes. "First, y'all sent us on a deadly mission to recover the melatonin cosmic tree. Now, y'all want us to go on another deadly mission to retrieve an ancient manuscript with spells and stuff?"

"Correct," says Father Time. "We have confidence that you can do it."

"Why don't y'all just send out a bulletin in the universe stating that we can recover anything that's missing," says Baker, skeptical about traveling to Monomotapa, Alkebulan.

Father Time and Mother Nature understand Baker's concern.

"You won't be alone," says Father Time, looking directly at Baker. "There's a group of rebels called Ujamaa's Loyalist Regime. We want you to join their ranks and help them defeat Ego and Deadra."

"What's in it for us?" asks Demus.

"Yeah. We're putting our lives on the line again!" says Baker.

Father Time replies, "We'll make each of you a demi-deity, a partially divine being with supernatural powers. Just let us know which specific powers you desire to have."

Baker and Demus look at each other. They can't believe what they are hearing.

"I want to be able to disappear anytime I want," says Baker, "and nothing can harm me when I'm invisible."

Father Time chants, "Om!"

Moments later, Baker disappears.

Barnes and Demus look around, but Baker is nowhere to be found.

"Baker!" Barnes yells.

"I'm right here," replies Baker, before reappearing. "That was super cool, man."

Baker disappears then reappears. He's feeling himself now.

Demus tells Father Time, "I want to be able to transform into anything I want. No matter what size, shape, or color it is."

Father Time chants, "Om!"

Moments later, Demus transforms into a colorful butterfly. He joyfully flies around the room and lands on the floor.

"Demus?" Baker doesn't understand Demus's transformation choice. "A butterfly? Why not a lion? A fire-breathing dragon? Or something more macho?"

Demus transforms back into his original form. "Wow," he says, "that was awesome."

Father Time and Mother Nature turn their attention to Barnes. He looks indecisive and doesn't know what powers he wants. The bluebird chime in his hand starts to shake on its own, and its echoing sound causes Barnes to realize what he desires the most. With confidence, he tells Father Time and Mother Nature, "I want the same power this chime has."

Father Time chants, "Om!"

Moments later, the chime transforms into a magnetic ring and wraps itself around Barnes's middle finger on his right hand. He is wowed by the ring's super attractive design, decorated with a glimmering black onyx stone.

The sound of an incoming train is heard. Everyone looks in the direction of the sound, but there's a metallic wall there—no signs of an incoming train or tracks. The sound ceases to exist, and Barnes is laughing. Baker and Demus feel duped. How could they not know that Barnes manufactured the train sound?

Baker tells Barnes, "That's dope you can manipulate sound."

Barnes replies, "I know, right?"

His ring is glowing. When he clenches his right hand to form a fist, the glow of his ring gets bigger and bigger.

"Your ring will become extraordinarily more powerful whenever you form a fist on your ring hand," Father Time tells Barnes. "But be very mindful because your ring has a conscience of its own. It is artificially intelligent. Therefore, think smart and use your imagination to communicate with it. Do you understand?"

"Yes."

"Think about what you want to accomplish and the ring will achieve it for you," continues Father Time.

Barnes clenches his right fist and points his ring at the ceiling. A tiny ball of energy discharges from the ring and morphs into thousands of descending dandelion seed pods.

Father Time and Mother Nature are pleased with the requests made by the three Black boys.

"When you arrive in Monomotapa, you will be teenagers and the same ages you were when you died on Earth," says Mother Nature.

Barnes, Demus, and Baker understand. They look outside. Through the windshield, they see several astropilots occupying a space station with the sun rotating in the background.

Baker asks, "What's that?"

"That's the sun," answers Father Time.

"Looks like there's a smaller one behind it," says Demus.

"The second sun serves as a backup generator," says Mother Nature. "Just in case the main one loses its magnetic powers."

A group of meteoroids crashes into the Mothership, causing it to wobble.

Barnes, Demus, and Baker are startled. After stability is maintained, Baker asks, "What was that?"

"Meteoroids," replies Mother Nature. "They're like stray bullets. Sometimes they come out of nowhere and hit the wrong target."

Barnes, Demus, and Baker look through the windshield and see a good number of spacecrafts spraying gold particles around a black planet.

Barnes asks, "What are they doing?"

Father Time answers, "Spraying a protective gold layer around Planet Black."

"Planet Black?" Demus scratches his head. "I've never heard of it."

"Planet Black is the home of the deities, our home," replies Mother Nature. "It cannot be seen from Earth's view because it's the same transparent color as space, full of light."

"But why are they spraying gold around it?" Baker asks.

"Gold is used as a protective shield," says Father Time. "Planet Black would be vulnerable to threats such as meteoroid showers if it wasn't protected by layers of gold."

"That brings us to our next problem," says Mother Nature. "It seems Ego has taken over our gold mine. He has deliberately put an end to any gold shipment heading to Planet Black. Now, we only have a small amount of gold left. If we don't receive a large shipment of gold soon, Planet Black will be destroyed during the next meteoroid shower."

The Mothership lands softly on Planet Black.

Mother Nature tells the three Black boys, "Go into the capital city. Maat will greet you and show you the way."

Barnes, Demus, and Baker nod their heads in agreement. Shortly afterward, they exit the Mothership. After entering the capital city, they see a large group of melanated divine beings approaching.

"Welcome to Memphis," says Maat, a healing deity, her pearly-white teeth sparkling like a diamond in the sun. Around her neck is a large choker-collared necklace made of pure gold.

Barnes, Demus, and Baker bow respectfully before Maat and her divine entourage. Barnes is extremely fond of Maat's beauty, and she realizes his glaring adoration when she gazes into his vulnerable eyes for the very first time.

"Come," she tells the three Black boys. "I will show you the way."

A short while later, the three Black boys are standing deep in the heart of the primordial thermal-spring waters, highly alkaline, with a pH of 10. They are wowed by the breathtaking waterfall view in front of them.

Maat takes her precious time to individually baptize Barnes, Demus, and Baker in the presence of all the deities living on Planet Black. No longer mere mortals anymore, the divine ritual transforms the three Black boys into demi-deities, and they feel supernatural powers surging through their energized bodies.

CHAPTER 3

Babita Harris is exiting a terminal at Monomotapa Global Airport, in Monomotapa, Alkebulan. She's thinking about Barnes. The last time she waved goodbye to him, he was standing inside a time machine. She steps foot outside, and the heat dislocates the thought of Barnes from her mind. For the first time, she feels the sub-Saharan warmth of Alkebulan.

"Lord have mercy," she says while absorbing the sun's rays. Her hair, rolled in a bun, is sandwiched under a fancy straw hat with flower trimmings. She cools her face with a handheld fan that's manufacturing more hot air than a cool breeze. Her luggage is seated upright against her shaved legs. "I'ma melt like butter in this furnace," she continues with sweat trickling down her face. "I thought it was hot in India but this is hot-hot."

"Mama Babita! Mama Babita!" shouts a dark-skinned man named Zulu Bello. He's standing behind a guardrail yelling, "Mama Babita!"

Babita locks eyes with Zulu. He signals for her to walk over to him. She does as she is told. On the move, she walks past a gang of Egomaniacs roughing up a muscular man. They noticed that the merchant doesn't have a barcode on his right hand, but he wants to sell his goods.

One of the Egomaniacs asks him, "Why isn't your hand barcoded?"

The man replies, "I am scheduled to get barcoded in a couple of days."

The Egomaniac who asked the question doesn't look too happy with the answer. Therefore, he rudely tells the man, "You can't sell at the airport if you don't have a barcode. No barcode, no work. Do you understand?"

The man nods his head and begins to pack his belongings.

Babita feels sorry for the merchant, but there's nothing she can do to help. Rules are rules, and who is she to tell the Monomotapans what they can or can't do in their own country. Therefore, she hurries away. At the guardrail, an Egomaniac checks her credentials. The pout-faced soldier allows Babita to walk over to the other side, where Zulu greets her with a huge hug and takes her luggage.

"Mama Babita," he tells her. "Welcome to Monomotapa, Alkebulan."

"Mama Babita, huh?" she replies. "I like how that sounds."

"Me too," says Zulu, his outfit wrapped tightly around his muscular body.

A new squad of Egomaniacs arrives on the scene.

Zulu suggests, "We should leave now."

Babita agrees. She follows Zulu's lead, and they walk over to his jeep, parked in the street.

Zulu opens the door for Babita.

"Thank you," she says before entering.

He closes the door, walks around his vehicle, and sits comfortably behind the steering wheel. After saying a quick prayer, he drives away from the airport.

Ten minutes into their travel, Babita breaks the ice, "Why so many soldiers at the airport?"

"Something bad must've happened," Zulu replies with his eyes glued on the dusty road.

Now Babita thinks she picked the wrong time to visit.

A short while later, Zulu drives her inside Monomotapa National Safari Park, home to thousands of wild animals.

Babita is astonished; her up close and personal encounter with Monomotapa's wildlife causes her eyes to water with tears. She rides past thousands of wildebeests, zebras, and gazelles.

"They're beautiful," she says.

Zulu agrees. He drives past a pride of lions resting on prairie grass.

"Monomotapa is an ideal spot for anyone who wants to connect with nature," says Zulu.

"And the air is so fresh here," says Babita, before closing her eyes. She inhales and exhales. When she opens her eyes, a group of giraffes is eating leaves from several trees. A short while later, she sees a family of elephants feeding on acacia bark.

"Who cleans up their poop?"

Zulu answers, "The dung disposal unit."

"They must get paid a lot," says Babita. "Waste management companies make a lot of money."

"Our dung disposal unit works for free."

"Free?" Babita laughs out loud. "They gotta be outta their poop-scooping minds. I know I ain't cleaning up no poop for free. That ain't happening. Not now, not tomorrow, not ever."

Zulu smiles. "Our poop disposal unit consists of dung beetles. Their purpose is to roll dung into balls. Some of them use the rolled-up dung as food, some bury it beneath the ground, and others live in it. They are the main reason why the air in the park is so fresh and clean."

"Wow," says Babita. "Guess I learned something new today."

"The world would be a better place if we allowed Mother Nature to have her way," says Zulu. "I don't understand why some people strive to remove nature from the human equation."

Babita sighs.

He drives her out of Monomotapa National Safari Park. A short while later, he parks his jeep in front of a large scrubland area, where a group of mountains is visible in the background.

Zulu exits his vehicle. He walks over to an automatic gate, disguised as a bush. He uncovers a hidden panel and pushes a button. Moments later, the gate opens.

Babita is shocked.

He makes his way back inside his vehicle and drives past the opened gate. It closes within a few seconds. He continues up a dirt road, causing dust to swirl in the air. Not too long after that, he maneuvers his jeep into a dense forest.

Salome McBryant Bello is looking out the kitchen window inside her fairy tale home. She smiles when she sees the jeep being parked and Babita sitting in the passenger seat. Salome hurries out of her home barefooted.

Zulu and Babita exit the jeep.

Salome greets Babita with a giant hug.

"Thanks for coming," she tells Babita. "I see you met my husband."

Babita looks at Zulu, shocked. "Your husband?"

He smiles.

Babita keeps it real. "He never mentioned you two were married. "I thought he was your…"

"Driver?" he finishes her statement.

"Yes," she admits.

Zulu pulls Salome close and wants the world to know, "I am everything to this beautiful woman. I'm her husband, her lover, her driver, and everything else."

Salome is embarrassed as Zulu picks her up and spins her around. Babita finds them amusingly cute as a couple.

"Put me down," begs Salome. "You're embarrassing me."

"Wait until tonight," says Zulu. "I'm going to embarrass you even more."

He puts her down. She's blushing and doesn't understand how Zulu always manages to find a way into her heart.

"You two have a lot of catching up to do," Zulu tells Babita and Salome. "I'ma leave y'all alone." He grabs Babita's luggage and disappears inside the house.

Salome and Babita are happy to be in each other's company once again. It's been almost two decades since they last saw one another.

Babita breaks the ice. "Looks like you've done pretty well for yourself."

Salome replies, "After burying my father, I sold his company and moved to Monomotapa. I wanted a fresh start."

"Trust me, I understand," says Babita. "After Barnes's death, I couldn't stand being alone. So I moved into my parent's home in India."

Salome admits, "I couldn't stand being alone either."

Babita concludes, "That explains Zulu."

"In a nutshell," says Salome. "Now, we're one big, happy family."

"You made the right decision," says Babita. "Monomotapa is a beautiful place. I am grateful to you and Zulu for bringing me here."

"No problem," says Salome. "And I'm sorry to hear about your parents. They were wonderful people."

"That's life," says Babita. "You never know when you're gonna go. They passed away while sleeping one night. In the morning, I found them cuddled in each other's arms."

"Come," says Salome, before grabbing Babita's hand. "I want to show you something."

Salome and Babita walk over to a rocky cliff. Ten meters below, they see a young girl swimming in a gorgeous blue-water lagoon.

Babita asks, "Who's that?"

"That's Nekaybaw. My 18-year-old daughter."

"You're a mother?"

"Yes."

"I had no idea," says Babita. "This trip has been filled with one big surprise after another."

Salome smiles.

"Barnes was her age when he died," says Babita, still traumatized by her son's untimely death. "They would've gotten along well."

Salome agrees.

* * *

Nekaybaw swims to shore wearing a swimsuit. She shakes the water from her body and gazes at the sun.

"May my future be as bright as yours," she says while absorbing the sun's cosmic energy. "May my days be as warm as your heart and may my nights be as kind as your soul."

A seagull lands on the sandbank. Nekaybaw imitates its movement. Then she sees two familiar people approaching.

"Sorry we're late," says Ninmah, a good-looking 18-year-old woman. She's wearing cut-up shorts over her swimsuit.

"What's new?" Nekaybaw replies jokingly.

"We're not that bad, are we?" Amara wants to know. She's the same age as Ninmah and equally as pretty. She's also wearing cut-up shorts over her swimsuit.

Nekaybaw shrugs.

Ninmah asks, "What's so important that you couldn't wait to tell us in person?"

"Guess who's a student at the University of Monomotapa?"

Ninmah says, "You're kidding me, right?"

"No," replies Nekaybaw. "My parents finally agreed to let me go."

Ninmah and Amara scream at the top of their lungs.

The frightened seagull flies away.

"That means we're going to be on the same cheerleading team," says Ninmah.

"We need to celebrate," says Amara.

"What do you have in mind?" Nekaybaw asks.

"The first one to grab a seashell from the bottom of the lagoon decides who's buying lunch," says Ninmah before stripping down to her swimsuit. She runs into the lagoon and dives in.

Amara takes off her shorts, runs into the lagoon, and dives in.

"That's not fair," says Nekaybaw. She runs into the lagoon and dives in after Ninmah and Amara. She swims to the bottom and sees her friends searching for seashells. A few moments later, Nekaybaw finds one lying under a plant. She grabs the seashell and shows it to Ninmah and Amara. The three friends swim to the surface. When their heads are above water, Nekaybaw declares, "Ninmah is buying lunch."

Ninmah splashes water in Nekaybaw's face before asking, "Falafel sandwiches at the vegetarian spot downtown?"

Nekaybaw replies, "That's not a bad idea."

The three friends swim to shore, where Ninmah and Amara put their shorts back on.

"The first one to your house is buying the drinks." Ninmah takes off running up a steep hill.

Nekaybaw shakes her head at her playful friend. She and Amara chase after Ninmah but they fail to reach the house first.

"You cheated," says Nekaybaw.

"Life isn't fair," replies Ninmah.

Amara is giggling. She enjoys being with Nekaybaw and Ninmah because they are extremely entertaining.

The three friends see Zulu approaching.

"Damn, your father is a handsome stallion," says Ninmah, licking her lips.

"Girl, you insane," says Nekaybaw.

"He's amazingly gorgeous," says Ninmah. "He reminds me of a superhero."

Nekaybaw exhales deeply.

"I'm serious," continues Ninmah. "He gives me that superhero type of vibe. You know what I'm saying?"

"No, I don't know what you're saying," Nekaybaw replies in a robotic voice. "Please don't tell him that to his face. He might start walking around here with a cape on."

"With no underwear on, I hope," says Ninmah, her imagination filthy like a sink filled with dirty dishes.

Nekaybaw replies, "That's gross!"

The three friends laugh out loud.

Zulu notices that three sets of lovely eyes are focused on him. So, he puts on his gentleman's charm. "I see you young ladies are having a great time."

Amara waves at Zulu.

"Yes, we are," Ninmah replies with goo-goo eyes. "And you look extremely attractive today, Mr. Bello."

"Well, thank you, Ninmah," replies Zulu. "You look exceptionally lovely also."

Ninmah blushes.

Nekaybaw shakes her head and changes the topic. "Where you going, Baba?"

Zulu replies, "I have to give a lecture. I'll be back later tonight."

"Be safe, Baba."

"I will," replies Zulu, before planting a kiss on Nekaybaw's forehead.

Ninmah is jealous, wishing for her forehead to also be blessed by Zulu's lips. When that doesn't happen, she is disappointed.

Zulu tells them, "I want y'all to stay in the mountains today."

Nekaybaw wants to know, "Why? We were just about to go to the falafel restaurant."

Zulu replies, "Downtown isn't too safe right now. There's a lot of military activities going on."

Nekaybaw, Ninmah, and Amara understand.

"Y'all have a productive day," says Zulu.

Ninmah replies, "You too, Mr. Bello."

"See you later," says Amara.

Zulu walks over to his jeep. Ninmah, Amara, and Nekaybaw wave goodbye to him as he drives away.

Nekaybaw clears her throat. "I wonder what's going on downtown."

Ninmah shrugs.

Nekaybaw opens the front door. In the living room, they see Salome and Babita conversing.

"Look who the cat dragged in," says Salome, her welcoming eyes filled with life.

Ninmah replies, "What's going on Mrs. Bello? It's been a while."

"Yes it has," replies Salome. "How are your parents?"

"They're fine."

"Amara," says Salome, "it's so nice to see you again."

"Likewise," says Amara.

Salome tells Ninmah, Amara, and Nekaybaw, "This is Mama Babita. She will be staying with us for a few weeks."

Nekaybaw, Amara, and Ninmah greet Babita.

She tells Nekaybaw, "You are the spitting image of your mother."

Nekaybaw agrees.

Ninmah walks over to an unfinished shawl draped over a vintage sewing machine. "Who's this beautiful shawl for?"

Salome replies, "It's for Mama Babita."

Babita is shocked; this is news to her. "Thank you."

Salome replies, "I was going to surprise you with it at the right time. I guess now is the right time."

Babita is pleased. This is one of the happiest moments of her life.

"You girls are in for a great treat," Salome tells Nekaybaw, Amara, and Ninmah, before signaling for them to have a seat. "I was just about to tell Mama Babita a famous Alkebulan folk story about Father Time and Mother Nature."

Nekaybaw, Amara, and Ninmah sit beside Babita.

Salome begins her story by saying, "Father Time and Mother Nature, and twenty-two other deities, created the first humans right here in Monomotapa. They inserted their spiritual laws and ancient spells into the brains of these primitive beings, who eventually became lords over Alkebulan.

The lords used the spells to create the first civilization. They built pyramids and cities and created math, science, astrology, and so on. They memorized the spells and practiced the spiritual laws to achieve great balance and stability. They knew one day they would have to recite it, verbatim.

"However, they made a crucial mistake. They recorded the laws and spells on papyri and titled it, The Hotep Brother Manuscript. Every day, they read its pages and realized the book was good. 'We should teach what's inside the manuscript to the people,' one of them suggested. The majority agreed. But under one condition. Only the spiritual laws would be taught, not the spells. The lords believed Alkebulan would sink into great chaos if the spells were known to the public. Those hungry for power would surely use it to control others. The following year, the lords began teaching the spiritual laws to the Alkebulans, and the people grew in wisdom, knowledge, and understanding.

"Centuries later, news of a foreign invasion surfaced. The lords buried The Hotep Brother Manuscript inside the Enchanted Forest, filled with giant trees, their tops reaching up to the heavens. When the armed invaders arrived, the book was nowhere to be found, and no one said a word. The lords acted like the manuscript never existed. They were hung, and many Alkebulans died that day. But The Hotep Brother Manuscript survived."

Nekaybaw asks, "Will Father Time and Mother Nature ever return?"

"I was told yes," says Salome. "But no one knows for sure the day or the hour of their return."

CHAPTER 4

Father Time and Mother Nature are standing on a runway next to a multi-tiered aerial vehicle. Two words, *Marvelous Falcon*, are engraved on the side of it. Several engineers are covering its body with solar panels.

Father Time admits, "The last time we flew the *Marvelous Falcon* was a hundred thousand years ago."

"I remember," says Mother Nature.

Father Time rubs the *Falcon's* chiseled body. He looks inside and sees Barnes, Demus, and Baker strapped in their seats. Father Time enters the *Falcon* and sits behind the main steering wheel. One of the engineers closes the door behind him. Mother Nature enters the Falcon and sits behind the co-pilot's steering wheel. An engineer closes the door behind her. Father Time activates the *Falcon*; its body illuminates with colorful lights.

The engineers slowly back up.

Father Time navigates the *Falcon* away from the launch station. He pushes a green button, which enables it to travel at the speed of light. A few moments later, it disappears into space. Father Time is like a child inside a video game system, having fun navigating the *Falcon*. He lowers the steering wheel, and the *Falcon* descends towards Earth.

Barnes, Demus, and Baker are amazed at the spectacular aerial view of Earth, even though they had seen it countless amount of times in their past life.

Mother Nature admits, "The first time we arrived on Earth, there were twenty-four of us. Twelve male deities and twelve female deities. And we saw nothing but water and not much land."

"We were desperately searching for gold," says Father Time, "and found lots of it buried beneath the ground in Alkebulan, where we eventually built an elaborate gold mine. We tried mining the gold ourselves but found the task too difficult and time-consuming for us to do alone. Therefore, we had to think fast about how we could obtain a workforce to mine the gold for us."

"At that time, I was in a committed relationship with Ego, Father Time's brother," says Mother Nature. "Ego was running things on Planet Black, and me and Father Time were handpicked by him to lead the search mission. Our assignment was to find gold in Alkebulan.

The search took longer than we expected, and over time, me and Father Time ended up bonding. Eventually, we fell in love with each other."

Barnes, Demus, and Baker are shocked. All along, they've been in the middle of a love triangle gone bad.

Father Time confesses, "We didn't plan on falling in love, it just happened naturally, and I was afraid. How could I tell my brother that the woman he loves was now in love with me, and I in love with her? So, we decided, once we got back to Planet Black, we would meet Ego face-to-face and tell him all about our relationship."

"And that's when a miracle occurred," says Mother Nature. "*The Most High, The Highest, The Universal Prime Creator* give us the blueprint on how to create the workforce we needed."

"We studied the blueprint for six days and six nights, along with the other twenty-two deities," says Father Time. "On the seventh day, we created the first man in my image, and he was to our liking. He couldn't move; his body was inactive. But *The Most High* sent a holy spirit to enter our inanimate creation. Moments later, the first man was brought to life, and we downloaded a portion of my essence into his spirit to give him personality."

"Is spirituality one of the main ingredients in experiencing life?" Baker asks.

"Yes," says Father Time. "Any life without spirituality is a dead life."

Mother Nature discloses the next phase of the creation story. "Shortly afterward, we created the first woman in my image, and she was to our liking. She couldn't move, so *The Most High* sent a holy spirit to enter her body. In no time, the first woman was brought to life, and we downloaded a portion of my essence into her spirit to give her personality."

"After that, we created eleven men in the image of the other eleven male deities. And eleven women in the image of the other eleven female deities. And each creation had the essence of the deity who provided them with personality. That day, our first workforce was created and we were happy to be in the presence of the world's first twelve couples. Each couple was assigned to the two deities who provided them with personality, and those two deities were responsible for providing provision and shelter for the couple. During this time, we showed the twelve couples how to mine gold for us, and how to rule over the fish of the sea, the birds of the sky, the animals, and every creeping thing. *The Most High* saw that what we had created was good. Therefore, the *Most High* blessed the couples and they became fruitful and multiplied. The twelve couples evolved into twelve large tribes, and they occupied Alkebulan. Each tribe worshipped the male and female deities responsible for giving them their personality."

"When word got back to Ego, he became very upset to hear that we created a human workforce without his knowledge," says Father Time. "We were the talk of Planet Black and Ego's enormous ego was damaged in the process. The fact that none of the humans were made in his image drove him insane. To this day, he hates us and the entire human race that we created. Looking back now, I think we were wrong. We should've included Ego in our plan to create a human workforce. If we did, the world would be at peace right now."

"What's done is done," says Mother Nature. "Water under the bridge."

"When Mother Nature and I finally told Ego about our relationship, he was past the point of jealousy," says Father Time. "To get even, he started dating Mother Nature's sister, Deadra, and they secretly went behind our backs and poisoned the minds of the sons and daughters of the twelve couples. They taught them to believe that life was all about gratifying themselves and to only worship the male deity and not the female deity. The humans listened to Ego's enticing dogma wholeheartedly and their egos developed and blossomed more and more like his. Eventually, the majority of them became independent-minded, with no regard for a collective society. To this day, the human race is still struggling to keep their egos in check."

The three Black boys are shaking their heads.

"Ego and Deadra came up with a brilliant plan to divide humanity," Father Time continues. "They managed to put each pair of deities, who created humans, at odds with each other. They did so by convincing the deities of each tribe that it would be in their best interest for each tribe to speak a unique language instead of all of humanity communicating in one universal dialect. Once that happened, humanity was separated within itself, and it has never been the same ever since then. Ego and Deadra were the first deities to use the divide-and-conquer strategy. Their concept was deceitful, and they knew it would spawn confusion, both in the deity and human realms. Eventually, the original human language disappeared over time and the twelve tribes found it difficult to understand each other. Therefore, communication between the tribes suffered massively. To add insult to injury, Ego and Deadra scattered the tribes all over the face of the earth, and humanity's unity was subsequently destroyed."

"After we found out what Ego and Deadra had done, we followed the proper channels and put them on trial for the crimes they had committed," says Mother Nature. "A jury of their divine peers found them guilty and they were severely punished for their actions. Ego was sentenced to 100,000 years, and forced to live in an isolated cave located inside a fiery realm known as the Devil's Lair. Deadra was also sentenced to 100,000 years, and put to sleep inside of a coffin buried inside a tomb on Earth."

Barnes, Demus, and Baker don't know what to say. This is perhaps the greatest story they ever had the privilege of hearing.

Father Time navigates the *Falcon* inside Earth's orbit. A short while later, he lands the spacecraft on the outskirts of Monomotapa, Alkebulan.

"A train will be coming through here soon," he tells Barnes, Baker, and Demus. "Take it to the last stop. Go to the University of Monomotapa. When you get there, locate a man named Profesa Mzima. He will tell you what to do next."

Barnes, Demus, and Baker understand. They exit the *Falcon* with their backpacks strapped around their shoulders.

Mother Nature tells them, "Good luck."

Barnes replies, "Thank you. We gonna do our best."

Demus and Baker nod in agreement.

Father Time navigates the *Falcon* towards the sky; it disappears behind the clouds.

Barnes, Demus, and Baker see a passenger train approaching. On the move, they grab hold of one of its cars. They climb to the top of it while fighting against the blistering wind. For an hour and a half, they travel on the train's top with their faces down and arms spread apart.

The train arrives at Downtown Monomotapa station; it's crowded with townspeople of all ages. Barnes, Demus, and Baker hop off the train's top without anyone noticing. They blend in with the Monomotapans walking toward the street, where

Barnes asks a nearby vendor, "Which way to the University of Monomotapa?"

The vendor, his right hand tattooed with a barcode, points east. Barnes, Demus, and Baker walk in that direction. They wander down the busy sidewalk, eyeing everything in sight. Along the way, they see a small group of townspeople crowded around a speaker.

"Our soldiers, who solemnly vowed to protect us from invaders, have pledged their allegiance to foreigners who murdered our beloved king and queen," Zulu tells the group of townspeople, who are murmuring among themselves.

Two members of Ujamaa's Loyalist Regime are standing next to Zulu, scanning the area for danger.

One of the townspeople asks, "What do you want us to do?"

Zulu replies, "Join the rebellion. Help us get rid of our enemies."

"Yesterday, one of the soldiers put this barcode on my right hand," says the merchant, before showing Zulu his barcoded hand. "And they imprisoned anyone who refused to get a barcode on their hand."

Zulu analyzes the merchant's tattoo and realizes that the Monomotapans are in the process of being productized.

"Look around you," the merchant continues. "We all have barcodes on our hands. If it wasn't that way, we wouldn't be able to buy, sell, or trade."

Zulu looks around and realizes the merchant is telling the truth.

"Two times today," the merchant continues, "soldiers came and scanned our hands with laser devices."

"That means time is running out," says Zulu. "We have to fight them now! Otherwise, we are doomed."

Barnes, Demus, and Baker are standing in the Crowd listening.

"But we will die if we fight," says an elderly townsman, leaning on a walking stick.

"He's right," says another townsperson. "We should act wisely."

"Think about our families," a townswoman suggests. "What will become of them if we die?"

The townspeople murmur among themselves.

"We don't have enough men."

"We don't have enough weapons."

"The soldiers are too many."

Zulu listens to the townspeople's excuses, one after another. He concludes their reasons for not wanting to fight are rooted in fear.

"You are right to think the way you do," he tells them. "But think about your ancestors. What would they do if they were here?"

The townspeople murmur among themselves again.

Zulu continues, "We can let the foreigners take what our ancestors died protecting, or we can die stopping them. Either way, we must make an important decision. Life or death? Freedom or captivity?"

A few of the townspeople agree, but many are skeptical.

A group of Egomaniacs burst on the scene, firing automatic weapons at his intended targets—Zulu and the two members of Ujamaa's Loyalist Regime. Bullets spiral through the air. Some whizz past Zulu's head and others travel through the heads and bodies of the two members loyal to Ujamaa. Both men tumble to their deaths.

Barnes and Demus take cover. Baker disappears before an incoming bullet can hit him. He reappears alongside Barnes and Demus. The scene is chaotic. Horrific screams fill the air while the townspeople scatter for cover.

Another group of Egomaniacs approaches from another direction.

Barnes warns Zulu, "More soldiers are coming."

Zulu sees that Barnes is telling the truth. "You have to get out of here," he tells Barnes. "If they catch you with me, they will think you are a member of Ujamaa's Loyalist Regime."

Barnes replies, "Can you help us get to the University of Monomotapa?"

"Okay," he tells the three Black boys. "Follow me."

Barnes, Demus, and Baker follow Zulu into a nearby alleyway.

Several Egomaniacs open fire, but their bullets miss hitting their evasive targets by inches.

Zulu and the three Black boys climb an iron fence and encounter a ferocious barking dog, chained to a fence. They escape through a conveniently opened back door. Inside a restaurant, they see many Monomotapans eating and drinking. They try their best to walk through without alarming anyone, but that doesn't happen.

Armed Egomaniacs enter. They see their targets walking away so they open fire. The Monomotapans in the restaurant duck for cover. Bullets enter walls, shatter windows, and kill a few innocent bystanders.

An incoming train is heard.

The Egomaniacs are distracted. They stop shooting and look around for where the train sound is coming from.

Zulu and the three Black boys escape through an opened window. On the move, they duck bullets while turning a street corner. Eventually, they make it to Zulu's jeep, which is parked in the street. Zulu sits behind the wheel, Barnes hops in the passenger seat, and Demus and Baker are seated in the back. Zulu drives away swiftly, leaving dust in the air. He breathes a sigh of relief because his rear-view mirror safely indicates that no one is pursuing them.

For the entire thirty-minute ride, they are quiet. Zulu pulls over to the side of the road.

"The university is two and a half miles in that direction," he tells the three Black boys while pointing to a large area of natural scrubland. "I can drive through there, but the terrain will be hazardous to my tires."

"We understand," says Barnes. "Thank you for bringing us this far."

The three Black boys exit the jeep.

Zulu drives away, leaving dust in the air.

Barnes, Demus, and Baker enter the scrubland. On the move, they walk past green vegetation.

"I have a feeling we'll see him again," says Barnes, referring to Zulu.

Baker replies, "I agree."

A short while later, the three Black boys arrive at the University of Monomotapa.

Barnes asks a student, "I'm looking for Profesa Mzima. Where can I find him?"

The young Monomotapan man points to a three-story building.

Barnes, Demus, and Baker enter the building. In the lobby, they walk over to a female clerk with a blossomed afro.

Barnes announces, "We're here to see Profesa Mzima."

She tells them, "The third floor. The second door to your right. He awaits your arrival."

Barnes, Demus, and Baker walk up the flight of stairs. On the third floor, they walk over to an office. Barnes knocks on the door.

"Come in," Profesa Mzima says.

Barnes opens the door.

Profesa Mzima, a man in his mid-fifties, is dressed in traditional Alkebulan attire. He tells them, "I thought you guys would never show up. Welcome to Monomotapa."

Barnes, Demus, and Baker take turns shaking Profesa Mzima's hand.

"I am an instructor here at the university," continues Profesa Mzima. "Also, the director of the foreign exchange program. And you guys are my foreign exchange students from Nubia, yes?"

"Yeah," says Barnes, playing along with the narrative.

Barnes and Demus nod in agreement. They left Earth as high schoolers and never imagined coming back as college students.

"Come," Profesa Mzima tells them. "Let's take a tour around the university."

Profesa Mzima leads the three Black boys out of his office, and eventually out of the building.

A shuttle bus arrives.

Profesa Mzima and the three Black boys make their way inside the bus. They ride around the campus for a short while, enjoying the scenery. Later, the driver transports them to a nearby dormitory.

"Come," says Profesa Mzima. "I will take you to your dorm room."

He exits the bus with the three Black boys following behind him.

CHAPTER 5

The next day, Nekaybaw is walking on campus with her backpack strapped over her shoulder. She sees Matata and a small group of Egomaniacs planting explosives on two old statues of King Ujamaa and The Queen.

Matata holds the detonator. He pushes its button, and a bunch of disappointed students watches Ujamaa's and The Queen's figurines being blown to pieces. The Egomaniacs celebrate by shouting. Two military trucks arrive hauling two newly chiseled statues of Ego and Deadra, both made of gold.

Nekaybaw sadly walks away and enters Monomotapa Cultural Center, where students are reluctantly walking to class. The destruction of Ujamaa's and The Queen's statues dampened their moods but doesn't stop them from living life as usual.

Nekaybaw walks down the crowded hallway, looking for a specific room number. She finds it and enters a full classroom with two recognizable faces, Ninmah's and Amara's. While walking over to her best friends, she sees Barnes, Demus, and Baker, seated by the aisle where she must pass.

Barnes and Nekaybaw make eye contact.

Nekaybaw is left blushing.

Barnes smiles as she walks past him.

"Who's that?" he whispers to Baker.

"Your guess is as good as mine."

Nekaybaw sits next to Ninmah, who whispers, "I think he likes you."

"Who?"

"The one you were eyeballing."

"But he doesn't even know me."

"Not yet," says Ninmah.

Nekaybaw replies, "I can't."

"Why not?"

Nekaybaw shrugs.

"You've been single for over a year now," says Ninmah. "It's time to meet someone new."

"And you think it's him?"

Nekaybaw and Ninmah look at Barnes; he's talking to Demus and Baker.

"Maybe?" says Ninmah.

Nekaybaw takes a deep breath and exhales. She knows she must come out of her shell and be more sociable. However, the thought of meeting someone new frightens her.

Profesa Mzima enters.

The students are attentive.

"Welcome to Kemetic Science," he tells them. "My name is Profesa Mzima. Today, I want us to get to know each other. This semester, we have three new foreign exchange students from Nubia and a couple of new students native to Monomotapa. When I point to you, kindly state your name."

He points to Barnes.

"Barnes."

He points to Demus.

"Demus."

He points to Demus.

"Baker."

He points to Nekaybaw.

"Nekaybaw."

When the student's introduction session is complete, Mzima begins to teach.

* * *

After class, while the students are exiting the room, Profesa Mzima stops Barnes, Demus, and Baker. He hands a piece of paper to Barnes.

Mzima tells him, "Go there."

Barnes looks at the address on the paper. Mzima tells him to memorize it. Barnes remembers the address.

Mzima tells him, "Swallow it."

"What?" Barnes is confused.

"The paper," says Mzima. "Swallow the paper."

Barnes rolls up the paper and swallows it.

"Good," says Mzima. "Tonight, I will meet you guys at that address."

Barnes, Demus, and Baker understand. They exit the classroom. In the hallway, they see Nekaybaw, Ninmah, and Amara walking not too far ahead.

Ninmah asks Nekaybaw, "When's your next class?"

Nekaybaw replies, "In five minutes."

"You're lucky," says Ninmah. "My next class starts in two hours. What should I do?"

"Maybe you should?"

"Shh," Ninmah tells Nekaybaw. "They're coming."

"Who?"

Nekaybaw turns and sees Barnes, Demus, and Baker walking up to them.

Barnes breaks the ice, "What's going on, ladies?"

Nekaybaw, Amaya, and Ninmah smile.

Ninmah replies, "Nothing much."

Baker introduces himself to Ninmah, "I'm Baker."

"I'm Ninmah."

Demus introduces himself to Amara, "I'm Demus."

"I'm Amara."

Barnes introduces himself to Nekaybaw, "I'm Barnes."

"I'm Nekaybaw."

"Can we meet later?" Barnes asks Nekaybaw. "Maybe after school?"

She replies, "I don't know. We are cheerleading at a rocketball game."

"Y'all should come," says Ninmah. "Rhinos versus Hippos; it's gonna be a classic match."

"We'll be there," says Barnes, while staring into Nekaybaw's seductive eyes. "I wouldn't miss it for the world."

Nekaybaw blushes.

"Aw shucks," she says after checking her watch. "I have to get to class. I'm running late."

She hurries down the hall.

Ninmah shrugs. "Guess I'll be seeing y'all later this evening, right?"

Baker replies, "That's for sure."

Demus and Barnes agree.

* * *

Later that evening, Barnes, Demus, and Baker enter a jam-packed gymnasium; they're lucky to find seats in the back. From an uncomfortable angle, they see Nekaybaw, Amara, and Ninmah on the sideline with the other cheerleaders practicing dance moves.

Barnes eyes Nekaybaw. Even though they just met, he has created a very special place in his heart for her. The one question that's bothering his soul, he asks Baker, "You think I got a shot with Nekaybaw?"

"Anything's possible," says Baker, his googly eyes focused on Ninmah, her tight cheerleading outfit is gorgeously wrapped around her slim body. "You just have to claim what's yours."

"Yo! What do y'all think about Amara?" Demus wants to know.

"She's cute," says Baker. "I give her that."

"Word," says Barnes.

"I'm thinking about stepping to her," says Demus, while observing Amara somersaulting. "I like her style, I think she's super dope."

Barnes and Baker agree.

* * *

On the rocketball court, the Monomotapa Rhinos, equipped with jetpacks, are warming-up at their basket. The Kemet Hippos, equipped with jetpacks, are doing fly-up drills at the other end of the court.

The referee, equipped with a jetpack, blows his whistle.

The cheerleaders take center court. Nekaybaw does a one-hand cartwheel into a full split. Ninmah does a backflip full twist. Amara somersaults and the Crowd goes bezerk.

"Let's go, Rhinos!" the cheerleaders shout.

The referee blows his whistle.

The Rhinos' cheerleaders retreat courtside.

Hashim Nzinga, the Rhinos' point guard, scores the first four baskets, putting the Rhinos ahead on the scorecard. The Hippos score the next six points. The action is back and forth.

Midway in the second quarter, Hashim is fouled harshly while flying towards the basket; he crashes to the floor in agony.

The Crowd boos. A shoving match breaks out between the two teams.

The front door bursts open with a boom.

A group of armed Egomaniacs enters the gymnasium. The players on the rocketball teams stop pushing each other, and the audience gets quiet.

Matata ushers in Profesa Mzima. His hands are tied behind his back. He and Matata walk to center court, where all eyes are on them.

Several large Egomaniacs take turns beating Profesa Mzima into unconsciousness.

"Let this be a lesson to anyone trying to join the Ujamaa's Loyalist Regime," Matata addresses the audience. "There's only one way this can end. Therefore, I urge any distractors to pledge their allegiance to King Ego and Queen Deadra now.

Because if you don't, we will find you, and you will receive the same treatment that Profesa Mzima got."

Mzima's bloody body is stretched out on the floor for all to see.

Barnes tries to get up, but Baker and Demus prevent him from doing so.

"Chill, bro," Demus tells Barnes. "We can't reveal our identity. Not yet."

Barnes realizes that Demus is right. However, it pains him to see Profesa Mzima down and out for the count.

A muscular Egomaniac picks up Mzima and carries him out of the gymnasium.

Matata orders everyone to leave. A short while later, the gym is empty.

Outside, the three Black boys see the muscular Egomaniac placing Mzima in the back of an armored truck. Another Egomaniac drives the truck away leaving dust in the air.

* * *

Hashim is conversing with Nekaybaw. Every time he tries to put his arm around her, she pushes his hand away.

"What's wrong?"

Nekaybaw replies, "We're not an item anymore. You broke up with me, remember?"

"You seeing someone?"

"No."

"Then what's the problem?"

He grabs Nekaybaw's hand. She yanks it away.

Hashim begs, "Give me another chance."

"I don't want to talk about this right now."

"Okay then, when?"

"I don't know. Maybe never."

Barnes walks over to the disgruntled ex-couple. He asks Nekaybaw, "Are you okay?"

She replies, "Yes."

Hashim feels disrespected. He tells Barnes, "Mind your business, or I'm going to beat it out of you."

Barnes doesn't take Hashim's threat too well. He balls his hands into tight fists and his ring glows. He's ready to unleash something terrible on Hashim when Nekaybaw steps in between them.

"He doesn't have anything to do with what's going on between us," she tells Hashim.

He replies, "Then you need to teach your friend a valuable lesson not to mingle in other people's business."

Nekaybaw tells Barnes, "It's okay, I'm good. Thank you. I got this under control."

"No problem," says Barnes; his eyes glued on Hashim before walking away. Seconds later, he takes part in a nearby conversation with Demus, Baker, Amara, and Ninmah.

CHAPTER 6

Schmeling flies into the Precinct of Ra via an opened window. "Caw! Caw! Caw!" he says while flapping his wings. He travels around the throne hall momentarily and eventually lands close to Ego's and Deadra's feet. He hops into his cage and sits on a cushion as if he is laying an egg.

Ego and Deadra are seated on their thrones, watching several Egomaniacs hauling in baskets filled with fresh quarried gold. The sight of the prized mineral brings enormous joy to Ego's and Deadra's hearts. They hold hands. Soon their objective will be completed when Planet Black is finally destroyed. In the meantime, it's satisfying to know that the gold shipments scheduled to be delivered to Planet Black have all been completely halted, and the gold is currently being stockpiled in a nearby warehouse connected to King's Mansion.

An Egomaniac blows an elephant tusk, and the entrance door slowly swings open.

A wounded Egomaniac enters. He limps over to Ego and Deadra with blood trickling out of several cuts on his body. "A group of rebels ambushed us on our way here. They killed a few of our soldiers and carried away the gold we were supposed to transport here."

Ego and Deadra are highly upset.

The elephant tusk echoes loudly again.

This time, Matata ushers in a battered and bruised Profesa Mzima. "Kneel before your new king and queen."

"Never!" Mzima answers and Matata beats him down to his knees.

Ego asks, "Who is this man?"

Matata replies, "A member of Ujamaa's Loyalist Regime. He's been posing as a college professor at the University of Monomotapa."

Mzima swallows blood. He knows his end is near. So he closes his eyes and prays to Father Time and Mother Nature for help.

Ego asks Matata, "Any success finding the rebels' compound?"

"No, but I have a feeling he knows."

Moments later, a surge of nitro-genic energy enters Profesa Mzima's body, and he is transformed into an Egomaniac. Shortly afterward, he tells Ego everything he knows about the rebels and where they are hiding. He lowers his head, and has no idea what he has done because he's under a spell.

Ego tells him, "You've done well."

Mzima smiles.

"Stand up."

Mzima does as he is told.

Ego signals for Schmeling to come over. Schmeling flies out of his cage and lands on Ego's shoulder.

"Tell the bird how to get to the rebels' compound."

Mzima reveals where the compound is located and the fastest way to get there.

Ego tells Schmeling, "Go. Tell us what you discover."

Schmeling flaps his wings and caws three times before flying through the opened window.

CHAPTER 7

Zulu walks around the rebels' undisclosed compound, located deep inside the mountains. At every turn, he greets members of Ujamaa's Loyalist Regime. He checks his watch and realizes he must go home soon. Salome and Nekaybaw must be worried about him.

"Twenty more minutes," he tells himself, before climbing a ladder. At the top, he looks outside the compound, but it's too dark to see. He refuses to use a spotlight because it might betray their location to their enemies.

Where could he be? Zulu wonders.

It's not in Profesa Mzima's nature to be late. There must be a good reason for his delay.

Shadowy figures are walking toward the compound.

Zulu wants to sound the alarm but chooses not to. He waits long enough to see Barnes, Demus, and Baker and recognizes them. He climbs down the ladder and signals for an armed rebel to open the entrance gate. The rebel does as he is told. Barnes, Demus, and Baker enter the compound and they are surprised to see Zulu again.

He asks them, "Were you followed?"

They reply, "No."

Zulu asks, "Who told y'all about this location?"

Barnes answers, "Profesa Mzima. He told us to meet him here. But earlier today, the soldiers beat him up badly and took him away."

"Where did they take him?" Zulu asks before scraping his face with the palm of his hand.

"I don't know," Barnes replies.

Zulu shakes his head. Deep down, he knows he might never see Profesa Mzima alive again.

"Welcome to the rebellion," he tells the three Black boys before shaking their hands. "We need all the help we can get."

Barnes, Demus, and Baker feel welcomed.

"So, where are you staying?"

Barnes replies, "At the university."

A truck with no headlights enters slowly through the opened front gate. A rebel named Solomon is driving the truck. He exits the vehicle with blood trickling down his right bicep. Several rebels hop out the back. Solomon greets Zulu and hands him a bag.

"Any casualties?" Zulu asks.

"A few of us didn't make it," answers Solomon. "But we managed to gun down a few soldiers."

Zulu opens the bag and sees pieces of mined gold.

"The rest is in the back of the truck," says Solomon. "We ambushed some soldiers while they were transporting gold to the Precinct of Ra."

"They will retaliate soon."

"And we will be waiting," says Solomon, grimacing from the pain shooting through his wounded arm.

"Go see about that cut before it gets infected."

Solomon agrees and walks away.

One of the rebels reverses a sporty, blue van and backs it up next to the truck. He exits the van and hands the key to Zulu before walking away.

Zulu turns to Barnes, Demus, and Baker. He hands the key to Barnes. "Use this van to travel back to the university. Bring it back tomorrow, at noon. We have an important meeting scheduled, so don't be late. All the rebels will be here."

Barnes responds, "We won't be late."

Demus and Baker agree.

Zulu tells the three Black boys the fastest way to reach their destination.

Barnes's ring glows and he senses that something is wrong, but he doesn't know what.

Schmeling, standing on a nearby tree branch, is eavesdropping and watching every move being made. He is positioned in the right place, and his black body is hidden well in the darkness of night. However, Barnes sees Schmeling staring at them, but thinks nothing of it. Schmeling flies away and disappears to a more secluded place where he can't be identified.

CHAPTER 8

The following day, the three Black boys walk past the newly erected statues of Ego and Deadra. More Egomaniacs than usual patrol the campus, a few of them harassing students.

Up ahead, Nekaybaw is walking by herself.

Barnes tells Demus and Baker, "I'll catch up with y'all later."

He jogs away.

Baker and Demus are happy to see Barnes talking to Nekaybaw. Soon, they hope to be in similar situations with Amara and Ninmah.

Barnes asks Nekaybaw, "Where you in a rush to?"

She replies, "Home."

"This early?"

"My class got canceled."

"How are you getting home?"

"The shuttle bus."

Barnes asks, "Mind if I ride with you?"

"No, not at all."

Nekaybaw asks, "Where are you heading to?"

"To visit someone special."

Nekaybaw assumes, "She's lucky."

Barnes replies, "How do you know the person is a she? Could be a he or an it."

"Maybe?"

"Why you say it like that?"

"I don't know," says Nekaybaw. "You seem like someone who cares."

"How do you know?"

"I don't," replies Nekaybaw. "But something inside of me tells me that you do."

"Your friends Amara and Ninmah told me some things about you."

"I hope they said some nice things," replies Nekaybaw.

"So far, yes."

"So far?" Nekaybaw laughs out loud. "You're funny."

Barnes replies, "I'm happy you find me amusing."

* * *

Hashim, standing not too far away, sees Barnes and Nekaybaw talking. His lips are chapped, yearning for her moist kiss, something he hasn't felt in a little over a year. Plus, it hurts him to see her wholeheartedly enjoying a passionate conversation with another man, even laughing at times. At this moment, Hashim becomes extremely jealous of Barnes and wishes to trade places with him. But the chances of that happening is slim. Therefore, he balls his hands into tight fists and vows to get even with Barnes, once and for all.

* * *

Barnes and Nekaybaw enter the shuttle bus. She finds a seat by the window and he sits next to her. The doors close and the bus begins to move. Barnes and Nekaybaw look at the passing scenery while riding away from the university.

Barnes asks, "Who was that guy harassing you yesterday?"

"My ex-boyfriend."

"I'm sorry to hear that."

"Don't be," says Nekaybaw.

"What attracted you to him anyway? He doesn't look like your type. His head is all big and stuff."

Nekaybaw laughs.

"Honestly, I don't know," she replies. "I guess I liked his muscles. I'm into guys with a lot of muscles."

Barnes flexes his muscles while Nekaybaw giggles.

"Enough about me," she says. "What about you? Do you have a girlfriend?"

"Nope."

"What type of girls are you into?" asks Nekaybaw. "Maybe I can hook you up."

"Someone humble. Someone who isn't self-centered. Someone with a good heart. Someone beautiful like you."

Nekaybaw blushes. "Is that original?"

"No, I only use it on girls I adore."

Nekaybaw smiles; she's impressed with Barnes's sense of humor and mannerisms.

He asks, "What's your ideal man?"

"A wise and kind person. Someone who respects himself and others. A family man. He has to have a sense of humor and be willing to love me unconditionally, forever."

"Forever?"

"Forever-ever and he has to be cool; he can't be corny. I'm not saying he has to be the best-looking guy in the world, but he can't be ugly either."

"I know exactly what you mean," says Barnes. "Sounds like you are describing me."

"Is that so?"

"I wouldn't mind being your boyfriend."

"You?"

"If not me then who?"

She exhales deeply. The steamy conversation is getting too hot for her to handle.

"Well, this is my stop. Funny how time flies when you're having fun."

Barnes holds her hand. "But the fun doesn't have to end here."

The bus stops.

He reluctantly lets go of Nekaybaw's hand.

She stands. "I hope you have fun with your special friend."

Barnes sighs as she exits. The doors close. She waves goodbye to Barnes, and he waves back.

The bus departs.

Barnes can't rationalize why he upped and followed behind Nekaybaw, knowing full well he didn't have anyone special to see. But being with her was worth the ride, and he enjoyed every moment of their conversation.

CHAPTER 9

The next day, the three Black boys are exiting Monomotapa Cultural Center. They see Nekaybaw and Hashim arguing. Barnes wants to walk over to the ex-couple, but Demus holds him back.

"Let them argue," says Demus.

"For real," says Baker. "That's none of your business."

Barnes knows Demus and Baker are right, so he keeps his cool. But he knows if Hashim lays a finger on Nekaybaw, he'll be right there to defend her.

* * *

Hashim tries to grab Nekaybaw's arm, but she pushes his hand away.

"I saw you getting on the bus with that guy yesterday," he tells her.

"So what?" she replies. "What's that got to do with you?"

"What's going on between y'all?"

"That's none of your business!"

Hashim grabs Nekaybaw's arm.

"Let me go," she says before freeing herself.

Hashim is offended. "So, it's like that, huh?"

"You made it like that."

He slaps her. Saliva and blood fly out of her mouth. She is hurt, offended, and embarrassed.

She tells him, "We're done!"

"I hate you!" he shouts in anger.

Nekaybaw's cheeks are blood red. Never in a million years did she ever imagine being humiliated like this. Her eyes are filled with tears.

Hashim goes through the motion of slapping Nekaybaw again. But this time, his blow doesn't reach its intended target.

Barnes catches Hashim's hand in midair and squeezes it. Hashim drops to his knees. Barnes wants to teach Hashim a valuable lesson for assaulting Nekaybaw. Therefore, he squeezes even harder, breaking all the bones in Hashim's hand. Hashim screams in agony, begging for Barnes to let go. But he doesn't let go.

Nekaybaw feels sorry for Hashim. Even though he disrespected her in the worst way, she doesn't wish harm on him. Therefore, she begs Barnes to let go of his hand.

He pays heed to her words and lets go of Hashim's hand.

Hashim stands and embarrassingly hurries away with tears in his eyes.

Nekaybaw tells Barnes, "Thank you."

"My pleasure."

She walks away. Barnes catches up to her. He tells her, "I can take you for a ride if you like."

"I didn't know you had a car."

"I don't actually," says Barnes. "But someone loaned us a van yesterday to get around. I can drive you in that."

Nekaybaw thinks about it for a few seconds. "Okay cool. I just need to get away from here."

"Where do you have in mind?"

"Anywhere but here."

Barnes tells her, "Gimme a second." He runs over to Demus and Baker. "I'm taking Nekaybaw for a ride. To help her get her mind right."

Baker replies, "You know we have to be at the rebels' compound at noon, right?"

"I know," says Barnes.

"But that's three hours away," says Demus.

"I'll be back way before then," says Barnes.

Demus and Baker shake their heads. They conclude that their brother is madly in love.

"If you're not back, then what?" Demus asks.

"Trust me, I will," says Barnes, before hurrying back over to Nekaybaw.

She asks him, "Is everything okay?"

"We're good to go."

Barnes and Nekaybaw walk away.

A few minutes later, he's driving the rebels' van with Nekaybaw in the passenger seat.

"Where to?" he asks.

"Don't know yet. I'll let you know."

Barnes drives away from the University of Monomotapa. His ring is glowing, and he senses that something is wrong. But he doesn't know what. He has no idea that Schmeling is following the van from above.

"Your ring is glowing beautifully," says Nekaybaw.

"It glows when something special is happening," Barnes explains. "And right now, we're happening. That's why it's glowing."

Nekaybaw smiles, feeling appreciated.

Barnes senses she needs more comforting. "Don't worry about that guy. He doesn't deserve you anyway. Just take it one day at a time. Eventually, the pain will go away."

Nekaybaw changes the subject. "I need to swim in a lagoon right about now."

"Just tell me how to get there."

"You make everything sound so simple."

"That's because life is simple. People just make it complicated."

Nekaybaw asks, "Why are you so kind to me?"

"I can be no other way towards you. You complete me."

Nekaybaw blushes. "Make this next left."

Barnes does as he is told. Ten minutes later, he's driving Nekaybaw past hundreds of zebras roaming a treeless grassland inside Monomotapa National Safari Park.

"It's not too far away from here," says Nekaybaw.

"You travel through here often?"

"Every day," Nekaybaw replies. "After my father picks me up from the bus stop, we travel through here to get home."

"That's awesome."

"You can park over there." Nekaybaw points to a scrubland area.

Barnes does as he is told.

Nekaybaw exits the van, and walks over to an automatic gate, disguised as a bush. She uncovers the hidden panel and pushes a green button. Moments later, the gate opens, and she makes her way back inside the van.

Barnes asks no questions. He drives the van through the opening and the portable bush closes moments afterward.

"The lagoon is straight ahead," Nekaybaw says before pointing to an ascending roadway.

"And my house is at the top of that hill over there."

Barnes scans the area and vaguely sees the top of a house a far distance away. Less than a minute later, he is parking the van, and they are exiting the vehicle simultaneously.

Nekaybaw and Barnes enter an attractive fruit garden, where he confesses, "Feels like paradise in here."

Nekaybaw agrees. "That's one of the perks of living in Monomotapa. We have a nice assortment of fresh fruits to choose from. You should try one."

Barnes picks a ripe berry. He cleans it on his shirt and eats it. "It tastes juicy and sweet just like you."

"How do you know how I taste and don't you ever say the wrong thing?"

"Everything about you is right and exact. I can't afford to be wrong."

She smiles. So far, Barnes has been a complete gentleman.

They casually walk over to the lagoon.

Nekaybaw asks, "Isn't she pretty?"

Barnes is amazed. "Extremely."

But he's looking at Nekaybaw and not the lagoon. When she realizes that Barnes is talking about her, she's embarrassed.

He plants a kiss on her lips.

She's shocked and takes a step back.

"What's wrong?" he asks.

"We shouldn't rush."

Barnes has no choice but to agree.

There's an awkward silence.

Nekaybaw breaks the ice, "I forget about my problems when I'm here. You know how to swim?"

"Does a zebra have stripes?"

"Then meet me at the bottom." She strips down to her swimming suit, runs into the lagoon, and dives in headfirst.

Barnes strips down to his boxer shorts, runs into the lagoon, and dives in after her. He swims to the bottom and sees Nekaybaw. They explore underwater for some time before retreating for air. After swimming to shore, they gather their clothes and travel to a secluded area surrounded by wild bushes and trees with big leaves. Hidden from anyone's view, they stare into each other's eyes for what seems like an eternity.

"You're beautiful," says Barnes.

Nekaybaw blushes.

Barnes kisses her again. This time, she kisses him back. Their lips lock, and they experience a brief moment of total bliss.

Nekaybaw asks, "Do you kiss all the girls like how you kissed me?"

"No."

"Because I've never been kissed like that before," Nekaybaw admits.

"There's more where that came from if you are interested."

"I am."

Barnes exhales deeply. Nekaybaw licks her lips and swallows saliva. He pulls her closer and kisses her neck. The thought of making love to Nekaybaw has become a reality. He lays her down on a bed of leaves and slowly removes the top portion of her swimming suit. What he sees, he will never forget. The sight of her breasts causes him to stare. They are developed like ripe mangoes hanging from a tree. He kisses between them and inhales her sweet body odor.

Nekaybaw opens her legs, ready to receive Barnes's erect phallus. He thrusts it inside her like a brute animal, and she moans as he drills her with his pleasure stick. Moments later, they are climaxing at the same time, sounding like two wildebeests in heat.

After her divine orgasm, Nekaybaw declares, "I hope this moment never ends."

Barnes agrees. He caresses her. This is the greatest moment of his demi-deity life. He looks into Nekaybaw's beautiful brown eyes and he can see a prosperous future with her.

"There's something I want to tell you," he says.

"What?"

"I'm nothing like the other guys."

"I know," says Nekaybaw, before kissing Barnes on the lips. "And that's a good thing."

"I'm serious."

"No, you're unique," says Nekaybaw. "And that's why I like you."

Barnes wants to tell Nekaybaw the truth about him being half-human and half-divine. But he doesn't know how to tell her. How will she react when she finds out the truth? The thought of that scares him because he doesn't want to lose her. But he knows, sooner or later, she's going to find out, one way or another. So why shouldn't he tell her now? So many thoughts are running through Barnes's mind that he takes a deep breath and exhales. His ring glows, but he doesn't know why it is glowing.

"Caw! Caw! Caw!" says Schmeling, before landing on a nearby tree branch. He doesn't see Barnes and Nekaybaw, but they see him flying away.

Nekaybaw takes a deep breath and exhales. A warming sensation travels throughout her body, and she feels something growing inside her womb.

* * *

Inside the Bellos' home, Salome and Babita are having a deep conversation about the political climate in Monomotapa.

Babita wants to know, "What will you do if things get worse?"

"I don't know," says Salome, deeply disturbed by the deaths of King Ujamaa and The Queen.

"Why not pack up and leave?"

"It's not that easy," says Salome.

"Why isn't it?"

"Zulu can't leave Monomotapa. He has obligations here."

"What about his family's safety?"

Salome exhales. She knows Babita is right. But Babita doesn't know that Zulu is a nationalist and the leader of Ujamaa's Loyalist Regime. Therefore, she wants to keep that a secret.

She admits, "I want to leave but not without my husband."

Babita understands.

The front door opens.

Salome announces, "Someone's home."

A fully clothed Nekaybaw and Barnes enter the living room. Salome is surprised because Nekaybaw has never brought a guy home before. She introduces Barnes and ends the introduction with, "My class got canceled so he gave me a ride home. I hope that's okay?"

Salome and Babita are standing there in total shock. They are speechless. Salome covers her mouth in disbelief.

"What?" asks Nekaybaw. "Can somebody say something?"

Babita, with tears streaming down her face, wants to know, "How is this even possible?"

Barnes, happy to see his mother again, walks over to Babita and gives her the biggest hug he can muster.

Nekaybaw is confused. She doesn't have a clue about what's going on. "They know each other? I don't understand."

Salome walks over to Nekaybaw and caresses her daughter. She logically concludes she shouldn't tell Nekaybaw that Barnes died 18-years-ago. That revelation might frighten her. Therefore, she only mentions, "That's his mother."

"His mother?"

"Yes," says Salome. "Isn't it wonderful how things come together to form a full circle?"

Nekaybaw agrees, but deep down within her soul, she thinks it's strange the way Babita is reacting to seeing Barnes like he was dead and now he's alive.

Babita holds on to Barnes for a little while longer. She doesn't want to ever let go of him, fearing he would disappear if she does.

"This trip has been filled with one big surprise after another," she says before wiping the tears slowly drizzling from her eyes. "Never in a million years would I imagine seeing you again. Especially, not in Monomotapa, and inside Salome's home."

Babita finally lets go of Barnes.

He is free to look around the room. "You have a beautiful home, Doctor McBryant."

"Thank you," says Salome. "So where are you staying?"

"At the University of Monomotapa," Barnes replies. "I'm staying in the campus dormitory with Demus and Baker."

Babita is shocked. "Baker and Demus, they're...?" Before she can say, "Alive," she sees Salome signaling for her not to say anything remotely close to the truth. At this moment, Babita takes Nekaybaw's feelings into deep consideration. At her age, she might not understand that Barnes is back from the dead. It might spook her out. Therefore, the less she knows, the better it would be for all parties involved.

"Yeah, we're foreign exchange students," says Barnes. "And Nekaybaw is in one of my classes. That's how we met and became friends."

Salome sees Nekaybaw giving Barnes that look, the one that a young woman gives to a young man when she is head-over-heels in love with him.

"Friends?"

"Yes mother, friends," says Nekaybaw, hoping her true feelings for Barnes are concealed.

Salome knows her daughter is hiding something important. But what? What is going on between her and Barnes that she isn't revealing? And how does that even work, Barnes and Nekaybaw together? The idea of them being an item frightens Salome because their relationship crosses into unfamiliar territory.

"It's time for me to leave now," says Barnes. "I have to pick up Demus and Baker. We have an important meeting we have to attend."

Barnes's ring starts to glow. He senses that something is wrong, but he doesn't know what.

An unmanned, laser-firing drone releases a hellfire missile that crash lands on the Bellos' gorgeous home. The explosive blast sends Barnes, Nekaybaw, Babita, and Salome flying into the next room, where they land in agony. The wood ceiling collapses and they are buried underneath fallen debris.

When the smoke clears, Barnes comes to his senses and easily removes the heavy wreckage from on top of him. He stands and looks around for Babita, Nekaybaw, and Salome. But he doesn't see them anywhere.

Someone yells, "Help!"

He follows the voice, and it leads him to Babita, buried under a heavy piece of lumber.

"Mom, are you okay?"

"It's gonna take more than a blast to kill me," says Babita.

Barnes smiles. He removes the lumber and helps Babita to her feet. Blood is running down her arms, and her face has minor cuts and bruises.

She asks, "What happened?"

"A missile exploded."

"Missile?" Babita says, shocked. "Who wants us dead?"

"I don't know."

They hear movements of someone fumbling through the wreckage.

"Over there," says Barnes, pointing to his right. They hurry there, to see Salome and Nekaybaw, trapped under a large piece of wood and other debris.

Barnes picks up the lumber and throws it to the side. Nekaybaw is amazed at how strong he is and remembers him crushing Hashim's hand. She and Salome stand; their heads and bodies showing minor cuts and bruises. Salome's right leg is bleeding and blood is trickling down her arm.

She asks, "What happened?"

Barnes answers, "We got hit by a missile."

"They know where we are," says Salome.

Babita asks, "Who?"

"The soldiers," Salome whispers.

Babita is afraid. She remembers how brutal the soldiers were at the airport.

"We're in danger," says Salome.

From a distance, they see Matata and a group of Egomaniacs approaching. Several of the soldiers have a rocket launcher strapped to their shoulders. On the move, they fire rockets at their intended targets.

A bunch of rockets whizz past Barnes, Salome, Babita, and Nekaybaw and crash into nearby walls. Salome, Barnes, Nekaybaw, and Babita duck for cover.

Salome says, "Follow me."

They have no choice but to agree.

She leads them into the next dilapidated room, where she tells Barnes, "Help me remove this rubble."

He does as he is told.

When the area is cleared, a floor hatch is uncovered. Salome lifts it. She looks below into darkness and then signals for the others to climb down the ladder. Salome travels down last and fastens the hatch lock.

* * *

Matata and the Egomaniacs enter the Bellos' home. Matata notices a trail of blood. He thinks someone must be wounded and follows the bloody trail into the next room. He looks around but sees no one. Walking towards a shattered wall, he steps on the floor hatch. His footing feels unusual, so he looks down and notices that the floor is uneven. He gets down on one knee and sticks his knife between the floor crack with precision. He jerks his knife back and forth and the floor hatch pops open.

* * *

Salome, Babita, Nekaybaw, and Barnes have their backs against a brick wall. They see sunlight gradually entering through the opened hatch. Salome bends down and grabs two grenades from a nearby utility box.

Babita is surprised. She asks Salome, "You know how to use that?"

"Not really."

Salome pockets the grenades, stands on her toes, and pulls down a huge flag of Monomotapan from the wall.

An escape tunnel is revealed.

"Hurry," Salome tells the others. "We don't have much time."

She leads them inside the dark tunnel, and their travel isn't long. Soon, they are standing on top of a rocky cliff, overlooking the lagoon.

Salome tells them, "We have to jump."

Babita doesn't look too confident. She can't remember the last time she jumped from this high up because she never did.

Salome asks her, "Can you swim?"

"In a pool."

Salome doesn't like Babita's answer too much. But there's nothing she can do now. Babita has no choice but to jump.

"Just relax," she tells Babita. "Jump feet first. Vertically. Your fall will only last a second before you plunge into the water."

Babita understands.

"Don't worry, Mom," Barnes tells her. "I'm here to make sure nothing bad happens to you."

His reassuring words give Babita the confidence she needs to make the jump. She looks at the lagoon one last time, controls her breathing, and mentally visualizes herself performing the dive successfully. With both eyes closed, she jumps feet first. Her free fall, lasting a little more than a second, disappears from her memory the moment she enters the lagoon with a moderate amount of splash.

Barnes, Nekaybaw, and Salome are looking down to see when Babita will come up from the bottom of the lagoon. After several seconds, she does and they are relieved.

Salome tells Nekaybaw to jump.

She dives headfirst into the lagoon with a little amount of splash.

Salome and Barnes look into each other's eyes for a little while.

"So tell me, what's going on between you and my daughter?"

Barnes is put in an uncomfortable situation. He realizes that Salome kinda knows about him and Nekaybaw, but not really.

"I just want to hear you say it. You owe me that much."

Barnes takes a deep breath. "I am in love with your daughter."

"Love? How is that even possible?"

"I don't know, but it is."

"When it's time for you to leave again, will you be taking her with you into the afterlife?"

At this moment, Barnes understands Salome's motherly concerns.

"I don't wanna lose my daughter."

Barnes never thought about what happens next. All this time he's been living in the moment and having fun with Nekaybaw. While assessing their situation, he hears Matata yelling, "They escaped through there!"

Salome tells Barnes to jump. "We can finish this conversation later."

"Not without you."

"There's something I have to do."

Barnes understands. But before he jumps into the lagoon, he manufactures the sound of machine-gun firings to buy him and Salome a little bit of time.

Matata and the rest of the Egomaniacs assume the rebels are shooting at them. Just to be safe, Matata momentarily puts a halt to their movements, while trying to properly access the situation at hand.

Salome takes out the grenades and breathes deeply. She tells herself, "I can do this!"

Matata, one of the greatest soldiers that Monomotapa has ever known, decides to find out how many rebels are shooting at them. Therefore, he cautiously advances and takes a sneak peek around the corner. But the rebels are nowhere to be found. All he sees is light at the end of the tunnel and Salome standing by herself. He doesn't know what to think of it. Why is she just standing there? And who is firing all the guns that he is hearing?

Salome uses her teeth to take the pins out of the grenades. While she is in the process of spitting them out, Matata realizes what Salome is about to do.

Therefore, he tells the Egomaniacs, "Get back!"

But it's too late.

Salome throws the grenades in the direction of where Matata was once standing. The heavy blast blows him and the rest of the Egomaniacs to fragments. Also, the eruption causes the ground beneath Salome to break. She loses her footing, and a substantial burst of fire blows her away.

Babita, Nekaybaw, and Barnes are waiting on the shore when they see the explosion and Salome's unconscious body falling and eventually splashing into the lagoon.

"Momma!" Nekaybaw says before covering her mouth with her hands.

Babita looks very uneasy. She doesn't know what to think. Therefore, she puts her hands in a praying position and starts to pray.

Barnes runs into the lagoon and dives in headfirst. He sees Salome's body slowly sinking to the bottom. He grabs it and brings her up to the surface.

Nekaybaw and Babita are happy to see Barnes walking towards them with Salome in his arms. He lays her down on the ground. But Salome isn't breathing. He gives her mouth-to-mouth resuscitation. Moments later, she vomits water and coughs.

Nekaybaw has tears in her eyes and some streaming down her face. Babita's eyes are also watery. Barnes exhales deeply. He knows they have dodged more than a bullet.

Nekaybaw helps Salome stand.

The first thing she does is thank Barnes for saving her life. Also, she's extremely grateful that she didn't sustain any major injuries, even though her back is aching.

"We have to get out of here," she says. "It isn't safe."

"We can use the van."

Nekaybaw agrees with Barnes. She leads them up the hill to where the van is parked, and they are thankful to find the van just how Barnes left it.

Nekaybaw, Babita, and Salome sit in the front bench seat alongside Barnes. He drives the van away from a place Babita and Nekaybaw once called home. Along the way, his ring glows, and he senses that something is wrong. What he doesn't know is Schmeling is flying high in the sky above the van, monitoring their every move.

"Caw! Caw! Caw!" says Schmeling while moving his beak to maneuver his body through the boisterous wind.

CHAPTER 10

Zulu impatiently walks back and forth inside the rebels' compound. He can't seem to stand still because his nerves are on edge. He has no idea that his home has been destroyed and his family is on the run.

"Where could they be?"

Solomon replies, "Probably on their way here now."

"I sure hope the Egomaniacs didn't capture them," says Zulu. Before he can entertain another negative thought, he sees Baker and Demus entering through the opened gate. He hurries over to them.

"Where's the van? And where's Barnes?"

They don't know how to answer Zulu's straight-forward questions correctly.

"He had to go somewhere and never came back to pick us up," says Baker, deciding not to mention the fact that Barnes left them stranded to drive Nekaybaw around in the van. Doing so will surely make Barnes sound irresponsible.

"Then we have to begin the meeting without him," says Zulu, hell-bent on starting on time.

Baker begs, "A few more minutes, please."

Demus adds, "He'll be here."

Zulu looks at his watch.

He tells Demus and Baker, "If he's not here in thirty minutes, we're starting the meeting without him."

They agree.

"Incoming vehicle!" shouts Solomon from an outlook post. He's looking through binoculars.

Zulu, Baker, and Demus hurry over to Solomon.

He tells them, "I see a man driving a blue van."

"That's Barnes," says Demus.

"I knew he would make it," Baker says joyfully.

Solomon confirms, "Three female passengers are traveling with him."

A short while later, Barnes is driving the blue van into the rebels' compound. He parks the vehicle not too far from Zulu, Demus, Baker, and Solomon.

Zulu is surprised to see Barnes exiting the van with his family and Mama Babita.

Salome hurries over to Zulu. He caresses her and kisses her bruised lips.

"What happened?"

"A drone dropped a missile on our home," Salome tells him. "And a bunch of soldiers tried to kill us."

Zulu runs the palm of his hand over his worried face.

"I didn't know where else to go," says Salome.

"You came to the right place," Zulu tells her. "We can always build another house. The most important thing is you, Nekaybaw, and Mama Babita is okay."

Salome agrees.

Nekaybaw walks over to her parents and wraps her arms around them. It's been a very long day for all of them.

Zulu points to Barnes. He wants to know, "How did he end up with you?"

All eyes are on Barnes. He wants to escape the spotlight, but he can't.

Nekaybaw answers, "He drove me home from school, Baba."

Zulu scratches his head. He puts two and two together and realizes his daughter is the reason why Barnes is late. He walks over to Barnes and asks, "Is there something you want to tell me?"

Barnes shakes his head. He doesn't know what to say. One thought occupies his mind—Nekaybaw is Zulu's daughter. If he knew, would he have still made love to her? He concludes, probably so. But what's done is done, and what happened at the lagoon had to stay at the lagoon. No one needed to know what happened except the two people involved.

Therefore, he tells Zulu, "Something happened at the university, and she needed a ride home. So I offered to drive her. When we arrived at your house, the missile landed a few minutes later, but we escaped. Now, here we are, safe at the compound."

Zulu senses there's more to Barnes's story that he isn't telling, but he doesn't know what exactly. Since he can't prove anything, he gives Barnes the benefit of the doubt. Also, he thanks Barnes for driving his family to safety.

Barnes looks up and sees a black crow flying above their heads. Many types of crows are solitary, so seeing one by itself is a normal sight in Monomotapa. His ring glows and he continues to eye the bird until it is out of sight. He's not too sure, but he's beginning to think that maybe it's not a coincidence that he's seeing all these black crows. Maybe it's the same bird he's been seeing over and over again. Maybe this bird followed them to the Bellos' home and it is responsible for revealing their location to the soldiers.

"Is something wrong?" Zulu asks Barnes.

"No," he says. "Everything is fine."

* * *

They walk over to a good number of rebels gathered by several drums filled with guns and ammunition.

Baker whispers to Barnes, "Looked like you and Zulu were having a really deep conversation back there."

Barnes replies with a smile and breathes a sigh of relief, knowing he just got off by the skin of his teeth.

Baker and Demus know something wonderful happened between Barnes and Nekaybaw, and they are eager to know what. However, now isn't the time and place for spilling tea. Therefore, they focus their attention on Zulu, currently standing on a podium, ready to address the audience.

"Hotep," he shouts.

The rebels reply, "Hotep!"

Zulu continues, "Earlier today, a drone missile destroyed my home, and my family escaped death by the narrowest of margins. Now, we have nowhere to go but here, with you."

The rebels shake their heads in disbelief and murmur among themselves. It's unfortunate what happened to Zulu's home, and the soldiers will surely have to pay for destroying it.

"Our enemies won't stop until Ujamaa's Loyalist Regime is eliminated," continues Zulu. "But we won't let that happen, will we?"

A rebel shouts, "Never!"

The rest of the rebels are murmuring.

"We will continue to fight the good fight until there aren't any more fights left to fight," says Zulu, using the right words to stir a burning fire within each rebel's heart.

An unmanned, laser-firing drone drops two hellfire missiles on the rebels' compound while they are pumping their fists and lifting their guns in the air. The explosions blow seventy-five percent of the rebels to fragments.

Zulu and Solomon tumble to the ground in agony. They are looking around trying to make sense of what just happened. The scene is chaotic and smoky. Therefore, their visibility is extremely blurry.

Somehow, Zulu sees Salome, Babita, and Nekaybaw huddled next to Barnes, Demus, and Baker. He thanks his lucky stars that his family is alive. Unconcerned about his safety, he hurries over to them.

"Follow me."

They agree.

Zulu leads Salome, Nekaybaw, and Babita over to a patch of brown grass. He searches inside the grass and finds a handle. With all his might, he lifts the handle, and a ladder leading into an underground bunker is revealed.

Salome, Babita, and Nekaybaw are looking down inside the bunker, and they see nothing but darkness.

"Hurry," says Zulu. "We don't have much time before the smoke clears."

Salome is reluctant to go first.

But Zulu offers her reassurance, "You will be safe down there. We built this bunker just for moments like this one."

Salome trusts Zulu. Therefore, she travels down the unstable ladder and successfully reaches the bottom. A short while later, Nekaybaw and Babita are reunited with Salome. They look up at Zulu one last time before he closes the access point to the bunker. Now the women are in total darkness, hoping for the light of day to shine upon them once again.

Above ground, Zulu hurries over to the three Black boys, Solomon, and several rebels who survived the explosions. Not too far away, they see an armored jeep with an opened top. Ego and Deadra are seated in the back and Profesa Mzima is positioned behind the steering wheel. A black cloud of nitro-genic energy is hovering above Ego and Deadra. Standing behind them is an army of Egomaniacs.

"It's Ego and Deadra," says Barnes.

"And Profesa Mzima," says Zulu, shocked to see Mzima alive.

The three Black boys are also surprised to see Mzima alive. They thought he was dead. However, they are more shocked to see the black cloud of nitro-genic energy entering the bodies of another group of rebels who also survived the explosions. After watching the rebels being transformed into Egomaniacs, they realized they have to retreat into the forest or else the same fate is going to happen to them.

"You, Solomon, and the remaining rebels should start heading into the forest," Barnes tells Zulu. "But hurry, we don't have much time left. Pretty soon that black cloud of energy will be making its way into the compound, and we can't be here when that happens."

"And that's what scares me," says Zulu, worrying about his family's and Babita's safety. "Won't it travel down into the bunker? I can't just leave them down there like that."

"You have no choice," says Barnes. "That's the safest place they can be right now."

Zulu takes a deep breath. He knows Barnes is right and exact.

"We can't afford to not make a move," says Barnes. "Standing still or being indecisive is harmful to our wellbeing."

Zulu agrees. In retreat, they can bait their enemies to follow them into the forest. If they are successful, then Salome, Nekaybaw, and Babita will be safe inside the bunker for the time being.

The three Black boys, Zulu, Solomon, and a handful of rebels are about to retreat when Barnes spots Schmeling landing on Ego's shoulder. At this moment, Barnes realizes that his intuition was right all along. The black crow that he saw at the compound not too long ago was the same crow that he saw at the lagoon. And this same crow has been spying on them and supplying important information about them to Ego and Deadra. Therefore, Barnes tells Zulu, "Y'all go. We'll catch up."

Zulu agrees, surprised to be taking orders from Barnes. A short while later, he and the rest of the rebels are retreating toward the forest.

* * *

Ego and Deadra are pleased to see the rebels' compound going up in smoke. This takeover was easier than they imagined. Now, they are moments away from destroying Ujamaa's Loyalist Regime.

Ego tells Schmeling, "Fly in there. Come back and tell us what you see."

"Caw! Caw! Caw!" replies Schmeling before flapping his wings and flying away.

Inside the rebels' compound, he flies around but finds difficulty seeing where he is going. There is heavy smoke everywhere and the rebels are nowhere to be found. As he tilts his wings to report back to Ego, a thick laser beam riddles his body. Everything immediately turns black, and

Schmeling falls into a steep dive, eventually crashing into the ground. He never saw it coming.

Barnes had Schmeling in his scope the entire time. "Gotcha," he says while releasing his clenched fist. Moments later, his ring ceases to glow. This is his first attempt at shooting a laser out of his ring, and he did it effortlessly like a skilled marksman.

Baker and Demus hurry over to Barnes.

"That was a great shot," Baker tells him.

"Thanks."

The three Black boys see a few Egomaniacs entering the compound.

With much urgency, Barnes tells Demus, "You have to do it now!"

Demus agrees. He picks up Schmeling's corpse and uploads Schmeling's entire essence into his body. Now he can talk and act just like Schmeling.

Barnes sticks his right hand out. Demus places his right hand on top of Barnes's right hand. Baker places his right hand on top of Demus's right hand. Together, they say, "Positive, Energy, Always, Creates, Elevation. (P.E.A.C.E.)!"

A few seconds later, Demus transforms into a black crow, the same size as Schmeling.

Barnes tells him, "Be safe."

Baker adds, "Yeah bro. You better come back to us in one piece."

"Caw! Caw! Caw!" Demus replies before flapping his wings and flying away.

Barnes picks up Schmeling's corpse and throws it very far away, where it can't be found. When it lands on the ground, the black crow transforms into Schmeling's original human body.

* * *

Ego and Deadra are anxiously waiting in the jeep for Schmeling's return.

Demus flies out of the smoky compound and lands on Ego's shoulder.

"Caw! Caw! Caw!" he says. "The rebels are getting away. You have to stop them now."

Ego orders Profesa Mzima to drive them into the compound, and he does. While there, they see a small group of rebels retreating into the forest. It's a triumphant moment, but Ego and Deadra would much rather see the rebels destroyed.

The cloud of nitro-genic energy hovers above the compound, following Ego's and Deadra's every move.

Ego exits the jeep and steps on the patch of brown grass. He has no clue that he is standing on the access point to the rebels' underground bunker.

Down below, Salome, Nekaybaw, and Babita are huddled together. They hear foot movements above but don't know who the foot movements belong to. Therefore, they keep quiet hoping their hiding place doesn't get discovered.

Profesa Mzima recognizes the access point to the bunker because he has visited the compound on many occasions. He tells Ego, "You are standing on the top of an underground bunker."

"What?"

Ego steps off the brown patch of grass he was once standing on and analyses the camouflaged item.

Demus is flying around the compound when he sees Profesa Mzima searching through the patch of brown grass for something. His worst fear comes alive when he sees Mzima pulling a handle and opening the bunker's top. Demus doesn't know what to do or how to stop them from finding Salome, Nekaybaw, and Babita.

Daylight shines into the bunker.

Salome, Nekaybaw, and Babita move several feet back so no one can see them. They hear Ego telling Mzima, "Search inside." The women are afraid because there's nothing they can do and no place they can hide. They are trapped and their ending is finally near.

At this moment, Salome sees a huge flag of Monomotapa covering one side of the wall. She didn't notice it before until the sunlight exposed it. She remembers a similar flag that covered the tunnel that they used to escape from the soldiers who tried killing them not too long ago. Following her intuition, she moves a small portion of the flag to the side and sees an escape tunnel behind it. Salome shakes her head and smiles. She knew Zulu wouldn't just leave them in a dead-end situation with no possible means of escape. Therefore, she's extremely grateful that their lives don't have to end inside a bunker.

Profesa Mzima takes his time to climb down the wobbly ladder. At the bottom of the bunker, he looks around for any sign of life but doesn't find anyone. This is Mzima's first time inside the bunker, so everything in there is brand new to him. He sees the flag of Monomotapa on the wall and thinks nothing of it. One last time, he looks around the bunker before putting an end to his search. He climbs up the ladder and tells Ego that the bunker is empty.

Demus, now standing on Ego's shoulder, is relieved to hear the good news. Somehow, Salome, Babita, and Nekaybaw escaped, but he doesn't know how they did it.

Inside the tunnel, Babita, Salome, and Nekaybaw are walking as fast as they can. Now and then, they turn to see if anyone is following them. But no one is. At a dead-end, they see a long ladder leading up. Salome climbs first, followed by Babita and Nekaybaw. On the ground, they see the army of Egomaniacs marching toward the forest with the nitro-genic cloud hovering above.

Nekaybaw, Salome, and Babita hurry over to the blue van that transported them to the compound.

Nekaybaw looks inside and sees that the key is still in the ignition.

Salome walks over to the back of the van. She opens the double doors and sees machine guns and ammunition.

Babita is exhausted. She sits on the ground and takes a moment to relax and calm her nerves. Her day has been filled with enough action and drama to last two consecutive lifetimes.

CHAPTER 11

Ujamaa's Loyalist Regime retreat as far as they can go, deep inside an old-growth forest. As they travel over timbered debris, they see countless large trees and standing dead trees, and sunlight barely reaching the forest floor.

"Let's stop here," says Zulu, scanning the area for danger.

The rebels agree.

Zulu sits down under a huge tree, takes a deep breath, and exhales; he's exhausted, and it shows.

A handful of rebels gather around him.

Zulu looks worried. If the soldiers didn't take their bait, then surely his family is in great danger.

He thinks about his wife and daughter and hopes they are okay. Also, Mama Babita, she must be alarmed, he assumes.

"We knew this day would come," he tells the attentive rebels. "Don't be discouraged because they are many and we are a few. It's not the size of the man in the fight but the size of the fight in the man. We have to use nature to our advantage. That's our only chance of winning and living to tell our posterity about this great day."

The small group of rebels pump their fists and lift their weapons in the air.

From a distance, they see two individuals approaching.

"Don't shoot," Zulu tells them. "It's Barnes and Baker."

They make their way over to the last remaining members of the Ujamaa's Loyalist Regime.

"Where's Demus?" Zulu asks.

"On a mission," Barnes answers without revealing too much. "What's your plan?"

Before Zulu can answer, an unmanned drone releases a hellfire missile that lands where the rebels are gathered. The explosive blast blows the rebels to fragments. Zulu and Solomon, the last two remaining rebels, tumble to the ground.

Zulu is in agony. His right leg is severely wounded.

Barnes and Baker hurry over to him.

Barnes tells Zulu, "You gonna be alright."

He nods in agreement, but the pain shooting through his right leg is unbearable; he's grimacing noticeably.

Barnes removes a knife from his waistband.

"What's that for?" Baker asks.

"There's a large piece of metal stuck in his leg," answers Barnes. "I gotta pull it out."

Zulu swallows; he knows he's about to experience additional pain.

Barnes makes a tiny incision inside the wound, and Zulu screams in agony. Barnes removes the metal from Zulu's leg, rips his T-shirt, and wraps it around Zulu's wound, preventing blood from leaking out.

Zulu breathes a sigh of relief, but he's still in severe pain.

Barnes helps him to his feet.

Zulu tries taking a step forward, but the pain is unbearable.

Barnes tells him, "You can do it."

Zulu grimaces. He knows he must walk or die. He chooses to live. He limps forward in agony, but the pain is excruciating. To take the pressure off his wounded leg, he favors the good one.

He tells Barnes, "I'll stay here and hold them back for as long as I can."

Barnes doesn't agree.

"That's out of the question. Salome and Nekaybaw are counting on you to stay alive."

Zulu knows Barnes is right. He won't last too long if he stays and fights against an army of Egomaniacs by himself.

Not too far away, they see a jeep approaching slowly. Profesa Mzima is driving. Ego and Deadra are sitting in the backseat. Demus, still disguised as Schmeling, is resting on Ego's shoulder. The army of Egomaniacs is walking behind the jeep. Also, the black cloud of nitrogenic energy is hovering above the jeep, following Ego's and Deadra's every move.

"Soon it will all be over," Ego tells Deadra, knowing the rebels have run out of places to hide.

* * *

Barnes, Baker, Zulu, and Solomon see Ego, Deadra, and the army of Egomaniacs approaching. Zulu and Solomon are worried;

being severely overmatched doesn't sit too well with them.

"We have to keep moving," Barnes tells them.

Zulu and Solomon agree.

Barnes, Baker, Solomon, and a limping Zulu, travel north to the end of the forest, where they encounter an enormous limestone wall, its length extending thousands of miles.

"What's behind the wall?" Barnes asks.

"Monomotapa National Safari Park," Zulu replies, still in pain.

Barnes remembers riding through the park with Nekaybaw.

"That's our only way out," says Zulu.

"But how are we going to get over this wall? Baker asks. "It looks like a mile high."

Everyone is looking up at the humungous wall.

"Probably is," says Zulu, scratching his head trying to figure out their next move.

"We have to go through the wall," says Barnes.

"But how?" Zulu asks. "This wall was built eons ago, and it will take something extraordinarily powerful to bore a hole through it."

Barnes's ring is glowing. He clenches his right fist and the glow gets bigger and bigger. Knowing exactly what to do, he points his ring at the wall and tells everyone, "Get back!"

They do as they are told.

A laser beam shoots out of Barnes's ring and bores a sizable hole through the wall, big enough to fit a truck through.

Zulu and Solomon are shocked. They had no clue that Barnes could utilize his ring to do such a thing. But now is not the time for them to ask intriguing questions about what just happened because the danger is still extremely hot on their heels. Therefore, they decide it would be wise to put great distance between them and their enemies.

Barnes, Baker, Solomon, and Zulu make their way through the newly formed hole and enter Monomotapa National Safari Park. They travel for fifteen minutes before stopping abruptly because Zulu can't continue any further. He's experiencing too much discomfort and doesn't want to put any more pressure on his wounded leg.

"Let's take a break and rest under that tree over there," he tells Barnes, Baker, and Solomon.

They agree because it pains them to watch Zulu limp from one spot to the next. No one dares to question his recommendation because they are exhausted themselves. A short while later, they are gathered under the baobab tree, its root-like branches are outstretched and reaching for the sky.

* * *

Profesa Mzima parks the jeep in front of the hole in the wall. Ego and Deadra, seated in the backseat, analyze the hole, and think what could have possibly caused it. What weapon do the rebels have in their possession that could bore a hole through a limestone wall in such little time?

"There's only one way of knowing what caused this," Ego tells Deadra.

"Whatever it is, we have to get our hands on it," she replies.

Ego agrees. He tells Profesa Mzima to drive the jeep through the hole in the wall.

Mzima does as he is told. It takes some time, but eventually, the jeep and all of the Egomaniacs are on the move inside Monomotapa National Safari Park. The black cloud of nitro-genic energy is still hovering above the jeep, following Ego's and Deadra's every move. Not too far ahead, they see Barnes, Baker, Solomon, and Zulu camped under the baobab tree.

Ego orders Profesa Mzima to stop the jeep.

Mzima does as he is told.

Ego licks his chops and assumes that victory is near. However, his joy disappears when he sees Barnes and Baker standing next to Zulu and Solomon. He remembers being crushingly defeated in the afterlife by Barnes and his sacred chime. Therefore, he looks to see if Barnes is carrying the chime, but he isn't. Also, the fear of being defeated by Barnes again sends a massive chill up Ego's spine as he continues to gaze at Barnes in disbelief.

"What's the matter with you?" Deadra asks Ego. "It's like you saw a ghost or something?"

"The three Black boys," says Ego.

"The who?"

"The three Black boys are here," says Ego, his mind racing a million miles per second. "But I only see two of them. Where's the other Black boy?"

"Caw! Caw! Caw!" says Demus while flapping his wings.

"I fought against the three Black boys in the afterlife," Ego tells Deadra with his fist clenched. "But Father Time and Mother Nature empowered them to overthrow me."

"Now you have them cornered," says Deadra. "You should strike them down now while the iron is still hot."

Ego agrees. With the Black boys out of the picture, final victory over the rebels will surely be obtained. Therefore, he orders his army of Egomaniacs to attack Barnes, Baker, Zulu, and Solomon.

The Egomaniacs charge forward and make their way over to their intended targets in record-breaking time.

Demus realizes that Barnes, Baker, Zulu, and Solomon are in great danger, but there's nothing he can do to help at the current moment. "Caw! Caw! Caw!" he says on Ego's shoulder while flapping his wings. He desperately wants to fly over to help Barnes and Baker, but wisely chooses not to because his mission will surely be jeopardized if he does that. Therefore, he aborts any ill-advised thoughts entering his bird brain.

* * *

Solomon has fear in his eyes when he sees the Egomaniacs approaching.

"Stand your ground!" Zulu tells Solomon before swallowing saliva.

Baker disappears.

Barnes clenches his fist.

Zulu and Solomon open fire. They managed to gun down several Egomaniacs before running out of bullets. But there are hundreds, maybe thousands of Egomaniacs swiftly moving in their direction. Therefore, they throw their useless weapons to the ground, expecting the worse.

Barnes's ring is glowing, and the glow is getting bigger and bigger. Bigger than it had gotten when it punctured that humungous hole through the limestone wall.

Barnes knows exactly what to do. This time, he tries something new. He aims his ring towards the ground. Moments later, it discharges blue energy that elongates itself into a protective shield that forms a dome around Barnes, Baker, Solomon, and Zulu.

The Egomaniacs open fire but none of their bullets can penetrate the shield, which is powered by the energy flowing out of Barnes's ring.

Zulu and Solomon can't believe what they are seeing.

"When were you going to tell us about your ring?" Zulu asks.

"I wasn't planning to," Barnes replies, while energy continues to pour out of his ring.

Zulu laughs. All this action made him forget about his wounded leg. But now he feels the pain again.

Baker reappears.

Zulu and Solomon look at Baker in astonishment. They wonder, how did he do that?

* * *

Ego and Deadra are viewing the suspenseful action in disbelief.

"How is this even possible?" Deadra asks.

Ego's silence is golden. He is extremely terrified because he knows Barnes possesses the power to defeat him again. Therefore, he realizes it would be in their best interest to retreat to King's Mansion. While there, he and Deadra can regroup and recite another spell in The Hotep Brother Manuscript to compete with the power that Barnes's ring possesses. As he motions to give the order for his Egomaniacs to retreat, he sees heavy dust rising to the sky. The ground shakes, but he can't imagine what is coming their way. What he sees is not what he had expected.

Thousands of wildebeests, buffalos, lions, elephants, and other wild animals are stampeding past Barnes, Baker, Zulu, and Solomon. The charging animals trample to death every Egomaniac standing in their path.

Ego senses that they are next in line to get flattened. Therefore, he controls the black cloud of nitro-genic energy to form a shield around the jeep—protecting him, Deadra, Demus, and Profesa Mzima from getting trampled.

The stampeding animals travel around the jeep before eventually escaping through the hole in the wall. Now, they are free to roam the forest like they used to do before humans arrived.

When the dust settles, Ego and Deadra look around; their entire army of Egomaniacs are no longer alive. Therefore, Ego orders Profesa Mzima to drive away from the battle scene because he doesn't want to risk losing the black cloud of nitro-genic energy.

Profesa Mzima does as he is told.

* * *

Barnes, Baker, Zulu, and Solomon can't believe what just happened. Never in their wildest dreams would they have imagined animals trampling an entire army of soldiers. In astonishment, they gaze at the dead Egomaniacs lying on the ground.

Barnes releases his clenched fist, and moments later, his ring stops empowering the protective shield surrounding them. The shield disappears and they are free to move around again. However, it's a bittersweet moment for

Barnes and Baker to see Ego and Deadra escaping. Even though the battle has been miraculously won, they know the war is still ongoing. Therefore, to ensure victory, they conclude that it would be in their best interest to follow Ego and Deadra because they will surely lead them directly to The Hotep Brother Manuscript.

"There's no way we can follow them on foot," Baker tells Barnes. "The jeep is moving too fast."

"Who said we had to follow on foot?"

Barnes and Baker are happy to see the blue van approaching and equally surprised to see Nekaybaw driving it.

She parks the jeep not too far away from the fallen Egomaniacs. Moments later, she exits the vehicle at the same time as Babita and Salome, and they are shocked to see so many corpses.

Salome hurries over to Zulu and hugs him.

"I'm happy you're alive," he tells her.

"Oh mine," she says. "You're hurt."

Zulu plants a wet kiss on Salome's lips.

"What happened here?"

Zulu explains the miraculous events of what happened to Salome.

Barnes gives Nekaybaw a heartfelt hug that lasts a little longer than expected. He wants to add a gentle kiss to the mix but decides not to. Now is not an appropriate time for him to show her passionate affection.

Instead of being upset, Zulu embraces the idea that Barnes and Nekaybaw like each other. But he doesn't know that their chemistry is much deeper than he thinks.

Nekaybaw feels nauseous and vomits.

Barnes caresses her. "Are you okay?"

"I'm fine," says Nekaybaw, a warming sensation traveling throughout her body, and she feels something growing inside her womb. "Just feeling a little bit queasy all of a sudden."

Salome knows this feeling all too well. She experienced it hours before finding out that she was pregnant with Nekaybaw. But she doesn't want to come to that conclusion, maybe not just yet. For all she knows, Nekaybaw's discomfort could have been caused by the trauma she has recently experienced.

Barnes's ring is glowing. He looks concerned. He wonders what could be wrong with Nekaybaw.

Babita gives him a hug and a little bit of reassurance. "She'll be fine. It's been a crazy last couple of hours."

Barnes agrees. He exhales deeply.

Babita is happy to see her son but didn't expect on seeing Baker.

"Nice to see you again, Mrs. Harris," Baker says before hugging Babita.

She smiles.

"Nice to see you again too, Baker." While looking around, she asks, "Where's Demus?"

Baker points to the jeep that's making its way through the hole in the wall.

"In that vehicle with those dangerous people?"

"Yes."

"We have to get him back," says Babita.

Baker and Barnes agree.

They enter the van with the engine still running. Barnes is seated behind the steering wheel.

"Y'all coming or what?" he tells Salome, Nekaybaw, Babita, Zulu, and Solomon.

"Of course we are," says Babita, her mouth sharper than a knife. "You're not leaving us here with all these vultures."

A large number of vultures are landing on the ground amongst the dead Egomaniacs.

Salome, Babita, Zulu, and Solomon happily squeeze their way into the back of the van, already filled with guns and ammunition. Spacing is tight but they manage to make it work.

Nekaybaw closes the back door. She walks over to the van's front passenger side and sits on the bench seat alongside Baker and Barnes.

After adjusting the rear-view mirror, Barnes drives the van away from the vultures feasting on the Egomaniacs' corpses.

CHAPTER 12

Meteoroids are crashing into Planet Black at an alarming rate of fifty thousand per hour. The protective shield around the black planet has less than an hour before it is destroyed. Some meteoroids are already flying through small openings and landing on Planet Black. Explosions at several locations cause a large group of deities to run for cover.

Mother Nature looks towards the sky, horrified at the damage being done. There's nothing she can do but watch the meteoroids explode against the depleting shield. Her guardian angels are standing nearby.

"Father Time, where are you?" To her surprise, she sees him maneuvering the *Marvelous Falcon* within the meteoroid shower. She's standing on pins and needles watching him evade death, knowing one wrong move can cause the *Falcon* to burst into flames. But Father Time is a master pilot.

A series of meteoroids crash into the *Falcon*, causing Father Time to bang his head against the steering wheel. The *Falcon* spins out of control, and Mother Nature covers her mouth with both hands. Father Time comes to himself and uses all his might to push the heavy steering wheel up. After gaining control, he flies the *Falcon* through a broken gateway and lands it on Planet Black.

Several astropilots hurry over to the *Falcon*, and soon, they are taking the gold out of it.

Father Time exits, blood trickling down the side of his head.

Mother Nature hurries over to him. They hug and kiss each other.

He tells her, "I found a small amount of gold on a nearby planet. But it's only enough to protect Planet Black for a few more hours. I have no choice, I have to travel to Earth. It's our only way of getting the right amount of gold we need to sustain us."

Mother Nature doesn't look too happy because Father Time might not return. If he does, she, or Planet Black, might not be there when he returns.

"Don't worry," he tells her. "I know how to stay alive."

The meteoroid shower is projected to last for three more days. If all hell is breaking loose now, she imagines what will happen on days two and three. She doesn't want to think about the horror, the catastrophe. Therefore, she realizes that Father Time has to travel back to Earth; if not, Planet Black will be destroyed.

"Let me go with you."

"No."

"Why?"

"I want you to be safe."

"Safe? Does it look safe here?"

Father Time looks around and realizes that Mother Nature has a good point.

"Wouldn't I be safer with you?"

Father Time thinks. She's right. Therefore, he agrees for Mother Nature to travel with him, and they enter the *Falcon*. An astropilot signals that all the gold has been removed, and they are cleared to takeoff. Father Time gives the pilot a thumbs-up before flying the *Falcon* through the gateway and into the heart of the incoming meteoroid shower.

CHAPTER 13

Profesa Mzima parks the jeep inside the Precinct of Ra, directly in front of King's Mansion. Ego and Deadra quickly exit the vehicle with Demus riding on Ego's shoulder. They are not surprised to see several royal guards standing there because they intentionally left them behind to guard The Hotep Brother Manuscript. On the move, Ego, Demus, Deadra, and Profesa Mzima enter King's Mansion, leaving the black cloud of nitro-genic energy to hover above it.

Inside, they see several royal guards standing beside The Hotep Brother Manuscript. Ego and

Deadra hurry over to the sacred book, positioned between their thrones.

Demus, still riding on Ego's shoulder, keeps his cool. He can't believe what he's seeing—The Hotep Brother Manuscript.

Ego picks it up and turns to page sixty-six. He wants him and Deadra to recite the 'apocalypse spell.' But halfway through the incantation, they are rudely interrupted.

Demus flies off Ego's shoulder, grabs the manuscript with his feet, and flies away. The book is kinda heavy but he manages to hold on to it with all his might. A short distance ahead, he sees an opened window and struggles to fly in that direction.

Ego is flabbergasted.

Deadra is also shocked.

Ego doesn't understand why Schmeling would do such a thing. But he doesn't know Schmeling is dead. The bird carrying The Hotep Brother

Manuscript is Demus, who is now several feet away from escaping through the opened window. Then it finally dawned on Ego where the missing Black boy was all this time. Right there on his shoulder and he didn't even know it.

"Shoot the bird before it escapes through the window!" he tells the royal guards.

They do as they are told.

Demus is almost at the windowsill when a bullet penetrates one of his wings. Unable to fly anymore, he lets go of The Hotep Brother Manuscript. Eventually, he lands harshly on the floor beside it.

Ego recovers the manuscript and looks at Demus twitching; his wing is broken.

Deadra picks Demus up.

They hear a commotion outside and machine guns firing.

Deadra inserts Demus inside her jacket pocket.

Ego tells the guards to join the other royal guards outside, and they do as they are told.

Ego and Deadra hurry over to the window. They see the blue van parked in front of the warehouse where their freshly mined gold is stockpiled. What they don't see is Salome, Nekaybaw, and Babita hiding in the back of the van, and an invisible Baker entering the warehouse. What they see is Zulu and Solomon firing rounds of ammunition at the royal guards defending King's Mansion from armed intruders. Also, they see Barnes standing several feet away from Zulu and Solomon. His ring, glowing enormously, discharges rounds of lasers at the royal guards firing bullets. Within a matter of seconds, the guards are no longer alive. Their burnt corpses are lying on the ground for all to see, and smoke is rising out of it.

Barnes, a limping Zulu, and Solomon are cautiously moving toward the entranceway while scanning the area for danger.

Ego and Deadra realize they must escape before it's too late. Therefore, Ego inserts The Hotep Brother Manuscript inside a military bag strapped around his body.

He tells Profesa Mzima, "Shoot anyone who comes through that door."

Mzima, still under a spell, agrees. He walks over to the front door and stands guard.

An invisible Baker, already inside King's Mansion, wraps his right arm around Mzima's throat and squeezes until Mzima is unconscious.

Ego and Deadra see Mzima falling to the floor. But they don't know why he passed out. Therefore, they hurry over to an iron ladder leading to the rooftop. Deadra climbs the ladder first and Ego is not too far behind.

Barnes, Zulu, and Solomon enter King's Mansion, where they see Baker reappearing over Profesa Mzima's body.

Deadra makes it to the rooftop, so they only see Ego climbing the ladder.

Barnes's ring is glowing, and he knows exactly what to do. He aims his ring at Ego, and moments later, it shoots several laser beams toward its intended target.

Ego is almost at the rooftop when he feels one of the lasers piercing his body. He yells in agony, not realizing that the laser has also cut the strap of the bag that was once wrapped around his body. While holding on to the ladder, Ego reaches as far as he can to grab hold of the descending bag, but it's out of his reach. The bag lands on the floor, and for a brief moment, Ego thinks about jumping down to retrieve it. However, he decides not to when he sees Barnes and Baker standing over the bag. Therefore, Ego continues his climb and joins Deadra on the rooftop.

Barnes picks up the bag and pulls out The Hotep Brother Manuscript.

Baker asks, "Is that what I think it is?"

Barnes's ring glows the same turquoise color that the manuscript is glowing.

"I believe so," says Barnes, happy that they have recovered the sacred manuscript.

Baker looks around. "Where's Demus?"

Barnes's ring glows a bluish color. "I think I know where he is."

Barnes puts the manuscript back inside the bag and ties the bag around his body.

"Do what you have to do," Zulu tells Barnes and Baker. "Solomon and I will go and check on Salome, Babita, and Nekaybaw."

Barnes and Baker agree. Seconds later, they are climbing the ladder.

On the rooftop, they see Ego and Deadra walking up a stairway leading into the black cloud of nitro-genic energy hovering above King's Mansion.

Barnes's ring is glowing and he knows exactly what to do. He aims it at Ego and Deadra. Soon, they will be no more. As he is about to shoot lasers out of his ring, he sees Deadra taking Demus out of her pocket.

"Wait, she has Demus," Baker tells Barnes.

Barnes realizes he can't shoot now because doing so will surely destroy Demus, whose body is currently being squeezed in Deadra's firm grasp. Therefore, Barnes is left with no choice but to abort his attack because getting Demus back safely is their top priority.

A hole in the sky opens, and the *Marvelous Falcon* flies through it.

Ego and Deadra see Father Time piloting the *Falcon* through the friendly sky. The mere sight of him angers Ego, to the point where he's foaming at the mouth.

"I can't believe he dared to bring her along for the ride," says Deadra, not too happy to see her sister riding inside the *Falcon*. It's been a long time since they last saw one another. "I can't wait to choke the life out of her."

"You will get your revenge soon," says Ego, feeling the same ill way about Father Time.

"And so will you," replies Deadra.

She hands Demus to Ego.

"Your arm is stronger than mine."

With all his might, Ego throws Demus as far away as he can throw him.

Barnes and Demus take their eyes off Ego and Deadra to focus their attention on Demus spiraling in the air like a football.

Barnes's ring shoots out an energy net that catches Demus before he can land harshly on the ground.

Barnes and Baker jump off the roof. On the ground, they hurry over to Demus; he's in critical condition, in desperate need of medical care.

The *Marvelous Falcon* lands not too far away from Barnes, Demus, and Baker. Moments later, Father Time and Mother Nature exit out of it and make their way over to Barnes and Baker. They shake their heads when they see the condition that Demus is in.

"We have to get him to Maat as soon as possible," says Mother Nature, concerned. "She can heal him inside the primordial thermal-spring waters. If not, he will lose his divine status and die a bird."

"What are we waiting for?" Barnes asks. "Let's get him there now."

"We can't at the current moment," says Father Time.

"But why?" asks Barnes, trying to get down to the nitty-gritty.

"The protective gold shield around Planet Black is depleting fast," replies Father Time. "If we don't get a shipment of gold there real soon, the planet, and the primordial waters, will be destroyed."

From a distance, Father Time and Mother Nature see Ego and Deadra entering the black cloud of nitro-genic energy. The two opposing duos stare at one another for a few seconds that seem like an eternity. The tension is felt by all parties involved in the stare-down. Moments later, the black cloud of nitro-genic energy vanishes into thin air.

Barnes removes The Hotep Brother Manuscript from the bag tied around his body and hands the sacred book to Father Time. "Maybe, this can help."

Father Time and Mother Nature can't believe their eyes. They thought Ego and Deadra escaped with the sacred manuscript, but they were wrong.

"Absolutely," says Father Time. "This will surely help our cause."

"Great," says Barnes, hopeful that maybe things will work out in their favor, and Demus will get the medical help that he so desperately needs.

"I saw a whole lot of gold inside that building over there," Baker tells Father Time and Mother Nature while pointing to the warehouse attached to King's Mansion.

* * *

Seconds later, Father Time, Mother Nature, Barnes, and Baker are entering the warehouse. Barnes is holding Demus in his hands. Father Time and Mother Nature are looking around, surprised to see so much gold stockpiled to the ceiling.

"This is more gold than we ever imagined finding," Father Time happily tells Mother Nature.

She agrees.

Father Time opens The Hotep Brother Manuscript to page ninety-nine. He and Mother Nature recite the 'Om spell' in their native tongue.

Moments later, the warehouse that they are standing in disappears, and live footage of what's happening on Planet Black appears in the sky. Thousands of meteoroids are crashing into the planet. The scene is chaotic. Deities are tumbling to the ground in agony and others are running for cover. Maat and other deities are huddled around the primordial thermal-spring waters, hoping for things not to end dramatically.

Father Time and Mother Nature put their telekinesis power to use by chanting "Om!" continuously. Moments later, the gold inside the warehouse magically travels upwards into outer space. Seconds later, the gold dissolves into tiny microscopic particles, and soon, a massively thick shield begins to form around Planet Black, protecting it from the incoming meteoroids.

Zulu, Solomon, Salome, Babita, and Nekaybaw are standing beside the blue van in amazement. They are wowed by the miracle taking place.

Father Time and Mother Nature are relieved to know that Planet Black is protected once again.

"We have to travel back now," Mother Nature tells Barnes.

"Wait," he says, before turning around and making eye contact with Nekaybaw. "There's someone I have to say goodbye to."

"Keep it brief," says Mother Nature. "Demus doesn't have long to live."

Barnes hands Demus to Mother Nature and walks away.

Nekaybaw meets him halfway.

"Who are these people you are with?"

"People?" Barnes giggles. "That's Father Time and Mother Nature."

Nekaybaw is shocked. She can't believe that Barnes personally knows two of the deities responsible for creating the first humans in Monomotapa.

"How do you know them?"

"That's what I was trying to tell you earlier that I'm not like other guys. I'm not from this world. Well, I used to be. But I died 18-years-ago. Now I'm part human and part divine."

"So, you're telling me I'm in love with a demi-deity?"

"Yes. I'm afraid so."

Nekaybaw takes a deep breath and exhales.

"I'm pregnant."

Barnes is shocked. Now he doesn't know how to tell Nekaybaw he's leaving.

"That's wonderful news," he says.

"Are you sure?"

"Of course," says Barnes, happy to know he is going to be a father soon.

He hugs Nekaybaw.

"I have to leave for a little while. But I will return as soon as I can."

"You have to leave now?" Nekaybaw doesn't understand.

"Yes, I have to go."

"But why?"

"Demus is dying. We have to take him back to Planet Black to save his life."

"Planet Black?"

"I will take you there one day."

Nekaybaw smiles. "I look forward to that."

"Me too."

"Is Demus also a demi-deity?"

"Yes."

Nekaybaw breathes.

"And Baker too?"

"Yes. We died on the same day."

"Wow. That's a lot of information to process."

"I know it is."

"How sure are you that you will return?"

"Very sure."

"How do you know?"

"Because you're carrying my baby."

Barnes rubs Nekaybaw's stomach.

His ring glows.

She smiles.

"The real question is how will you break the news to your parents?"

"Don't know yet. I think my mother knows something is going on between us. So I will probably tell her first."

"Good idea," says Barnes.

With all eyes on them, they kiss.

"I love you."

"I love you too," says Nekaybaw.

Barnes walks away.

Nekaybaw walks over to Salome, Babita, Zulu, and Solomon with tears in her eyes. Salome caresses Nekaybaw, and they see Barnes entering the *Marvelous Falcon*. Moments later, the *Falcon* flies into outer space and disappears beyond the clouds.

* * *

The *Falcon* lands on Planet Black, where a multitude of deities is gathered.

Father Time, Mother Nature, Barnes, and Baker exit the *Falcon* to thunderous applauds. Barnes is carrying Demus in his hand. With no time to waste, they hurry over to the primordial thermal-spring waters, where Maat is waiting for them.

She receives a dying Demus from Barnes.

"Please, help him," he tells her.

"I will do what I can."

Maat carries Demus deep into the heart of the primordial thermal-spring waters, where he is submerged for thirty seconds. Underwater, a restoration occurs, and Demus is miraculously healed.

Maat brings Demus to the surface. He shakes himself in the palm of her hands and vibrates his wings to get rid of the excess water on his body. Moments later, he joyfully flies away and lands near Barnes and Baker. Demus returns to his original self, and he is extremely happy and grateful for the opportunity to feel his head and body once again.

Barnes and Baker take turns hugging Demus. They could've lost him forever, but they didn't. And because of that, they are thankful.

Barnes sticks his right hand out. Demus places his right hand on top of Barnes's right hand. Baker places his right hand on top of Demus's right hand. Together, they say, "Positive, Energy, Always, Creates, Elevation. (P.E.A.C.E.)!"

* * *

Three months later, Zulu enters King's Mansion wearing a black gown. He walks over to a golden baptismal font with all eyes on him.

Ptah, a newly appointed High Priest of Monomotapa, greets Zulu with a firm handshake. His clergymen, standing nearby, bow to show respect to Zulu.

Babita, Nekaybaw, Ninmah, and Amara are seated in the front row, watching the coronation.

Nekaybaw's baby bump is visible and she has gained a good amount of weight.

The rest of the mansion is occupied with townspeople, natives of Monomotapa.

Zulu steps inside the baptismal font. Ptah plunges Zulu's head and body underwater. Moments later, Zulu is lifted out of the water.

Ptah tells him, "You are now the new King of Monomotapa, Alkebulan."

Zulu is happy.

The audience cheers loudly.

Two male ushers, holding a veil, walk over to Zulu. They hide him from public view, and he changes into a purple robe with gold trimmings.

Soft moccasins are placed on his feet, and a long staff is given to him to hold. The ushers remove the veil.

Ptah places the King's Crown on Zulu's head, and the audience cheers again.

A group of musicians plays various instruments.

The festive sound ceases when Salome enters King's Mansion wearing a black gown. She walks over to the baptismal font with all eyes are on her.

Ptah greets Salome with a firm handshake. His clergymen, standing nearby, bow to show respect to Salome. She steps inside the baptismal font. Ptah plunges her head and body underwater. Moments later, Salome is lifted out of the water.

Ptah tells her, "You are now the new Queen of Monomotapa."

Salome is happy.

The audience cheers loudly.

Two female ushers, holding a veil, walk over to Salome. They hide her from public view, and she changes into a lavender robe with pink trimmings. Soft moccasins are placed on her feet.

The ushers remove the veil.

Ptah places the Queen's Crown on Salome's head and the audience cheers again.

Musicians play instruments while Zulu and Salome are seated on their thrones. They are extremely happy. Never in their wildest dreams would they have imagined being the rightful rulers of Monomotapa, Alkebulan.

The End.

SALUTATIONS:

Hotep to The Most-High The Highest The Universal Prime Creator for giving me the right wisdom, knowledge, and understanding to finish writing this sequel. Also, I want to thank my family and friends for their continuous love and support. Peace.

About the Author

Zangba Thomson is an award-winning author, journalist, screenwriter, recording artist, and founder/Editor-in-Chief at Bong Mines Entertainment. His creative works deal mainly in the realms of spirituality, metaphysics, and visionary, with lots of love and drama sprinkled in between. His creations have been seen on or talked about in major media outlets such as FOX 5, NBC, Today, Fox & Friends, Kathy Lee & Hoda, ABC, Vibe Magazine, Centric TV, HOT 97, Essence Magazine, and many more.

Alongside his *Three Black Boys* book series, Thomson has co-written other books such as *Do Right Do Good*, a guidebook to vision-fulfillment and entrepreneurship, endorsed by Russell Simmons and Dr. Dennis Kimbro; and the urban, bestselling relationship book, *Single Man, Married Man*. Thomson's latest success guidebook, entitled "Take a Look... There's Money All Around You!" highlights the secret keys to becoming a prosperous moneymaking machine.

On July 31, 2016, at the National Black Theatre in Harlem, New York, Thomson received the *Bai T. Moore Literary Award* during a ceremony commemorating the 169th Anniversary of Liberian Independence. That night, he also received a Certificate of Special Congressional Recognition from Charles Bernard Rangel for his literary achievements, commitment to strengthening our Nation, and making a difference through volunteering service in urban communities.

Zangba Thomson + Photo by Ishmel Twice

Twitter: @zangbathomson
Facebook: @iLikeZangba
Instagram: @zangba

Book One

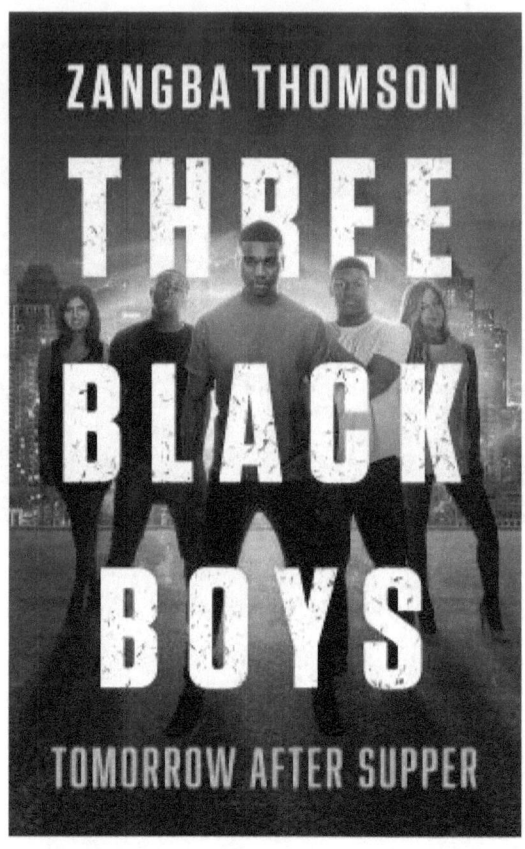

"Thomson's ear for street-slang vernacular is effective in bringing his characters to life and creates a chillingly real backdrop." – **Kirkus Discoveries Review**

"Take a Look…There's Money All Around You!" is a must-have, straightforward, and easy to understand guidebook that highlights the secret ingredients needed to become a prosperous moneymaking machine.

"Hip-Hop, Soul, and R&B" is a wonderful six-track EP by ZANGBA featuring Maskerade. The likable project contains relationship-based narratives, ear-welcoming vocals, and conversational rap lyrics. Also, the EP possesses melodic instrumentations flavored with hip-hop, modern soul, and contemporary R&B elements.

Ma Benson's original *"Whipped Body Butter"* has healed countless amounts of dry and troubled skin because of its 100% all-natural and empowering ingredients, ideal for moisturizing skin, body, and hair.

Materials: Avocado Oil, Pomegranate Seed Oil, Jasmine Fragrance Oil, Yellow Beeswax, Arrowroot Powder, Virgin Shea Nut Butter, Extra Virgin Organic Coconut Oil, Virgin Organic Argan Nut Oil, Organic Jojoba Oil, Castor Oil, Organic Lavender Oil, and Sweet Virgin Organic Almond Oil.

Order at **www.etsy.com/shop/MaBproducts.**